With best Compliments
Embassy of India, Berne

Lengdon's Legacy
Tai Khamti Folktales from Arunachal Pradesh

Folklore Series

Lengdon's Legacy
Tai Khamti Folktales from Arunachal Pradesh

Retold with Illustrations by
Tertia Sandhu

NATIONAL BOOK TRUST, INDIA

ISBN 978-81-237-5795-7

First Edition 2010
First Reprint 2011
Second Reprint 2015 (*Saka* 1936)
© Tertia Sandhu, 2010
₹ 130.00
Published by the Director, National Book Trust, India
Nehru Bhawan, 5 Institutional Area, Phase-II
Vasant Kunj, New Delhi-110 070
www.nbtindia.gov.in

Contents

	Introduction	vii
1.	Lengdon's Legacy	1
2.	Nang Chanta Looks for a Groom	5
3.	Yae Sengchi Esengtum	9
4.	Ai Khan	20
5.	Nang Pham & the Three Suitors	28
6.	Wo Pem Samlo	34
7.	The Milky Way	37
8.	Ai Khai Ngup	45
9.	Nang Champu & Chow Manong	52
10.	The Three Answers	57
11.	The Coconut Fairy	65
12.	Phanthoi & Tiger	73
13.	Poo's Wisdom	78
14.	Phanthoi Outwits the Villagers	84
15.	Sangken	86
16.	Devotion	91
17.	The Dragon Princess	94
18.	Bramawati & Nang Kungtra	98
19.	The First Yasi	106
20.	The Turtle Prince	110
21.	Chow Ai & the Phephai	117

22.	The Golden Tree	123
23.	How the Tiger Got its Stripes	127
24.	Chow Pingya & Nang Samati	130
25.	The Manang Tree	137
26.	Mok Phet the Liar	141
27.	Chow Dhammasethe	144
28.	The Man Nobody Wanted	149
29.	Spirit of the Mit	154
30.	Gold or Grain	157
31.	Mokmo & the Prince	162
32.	Ai Mao, Ngee Hunangyow & Sam Songpha	170
33.	Along Cham Kam	178
34.	Kemisanta & Chow Naracheta	184
35.	Luk-Khoi the Son-in-law	190
36.	The Good Wife	194
37.	Pona Changsang & the Spirit Judge	198
38.	Chow Nong Long, Master of the Great Lake	201
39.	The Man Who Ate Three Pots of Rice	205
40.	Chow Amasa	210
41.	The Hunter & the Monks	213
42.	One Kilo Salt for One Gooseberry	215
43.	Pakkham the Jinx	220

Legends/Beliefs/Rituals   223

Introduction

The Tai Khamtis of the Lohit district of Arunachal Pradesh and North Lakhimpur in upper Assam are a branch of the great 'Tai' or 'Shan' race of Southeast Asia and trace their origin to Western China.

By Tai people, we mean the Thai, the Lao, the Shan, the Dai and the Tai. Tai people have preserved in their folk tales and tradition a sense of common origin, which is evident in their language and culture. Despite variations in dialect and accents over the years leading to their divergence, there still is some degree of mutual understanding among them.

'Tai' first appeared in Chinese history in Shanzi and Honan as early as BC 2515[1] and was the only hereditary title of rank enjoyed by the highest aristocracy in ancient China. Thus, Tai means a respectable and independent personage in address, implying great power and hence political freedom from subjection. The first kingdom of the Tai in recorded history was the Tsu Kingdom, which was established between BC 2000 and 1500.[2]

Khamti means 'Land of Gold' (Kham-gold, Ti-place), the region being said to be extremely rich in gold. The Tai who settled in Khamti Long in the fourteenth century at Putao on the banks

---

1. *The Tai Khamti*, Lila Gogoi (Comp.), Chowkhamoon Gohain (Namssom), 1971, Chowkham, NEFA, p. 6.
2. *Origin of Tai Ahoms* (Part I), Ashim Borgohain, http://taiohominternational.org

of the Nam Kiu river (Irrawaddy) themselves came to be known as Khamti.

They migrated to Assam in the later half of the 18th century from Khamti Long in Northern Myanmar and settled along the Tengapani river near Sadiya, with the sanction of the Ahom kings. Later on, they ousted the reigning Ahom Governor known as the 'Sadiya Khuwa Gohain' and usurped his title, reducing the local Assamese to slavery. The Assam Government being too weak to resist, acknowledged the Khamti chief as 'Sadiya Khuwa Gohain'.

With the annexation of Sadiya to the British colonial administration, the Khamtis migrated to other parts of the North Eastern region in early 1869. According to a treaty signed between the British and the Khamtis, the Khamtis were empowered to rule the areas in the foothills of the Himalayas, east of Kundil Mukh, in return for their allegiance and help to the British in case of foreign invasion from the Southeast.

The majority of the Khamtis led by their chief Chow Phahom Namsoam, settled near the Tengapani river (Nam soam or sour water) where he built a Buddhist temple covered in gold leaf. The village derived its name from the golden temple and came to be known as Chongkham (Golden temple). The Khamtis are divided into innumerable clans, each clan having its own village and Chowpha (king) and the size of the village depending on the strength of the clan.

They are followers of Theravada Buddhism (Hinayana) and each village has a Chong (temple), a Kongmu (pagoda) and resident monks who double up as teachers, teaching the youth to read and write in the Tai and Pali script. Monks play an important role in the community and are highly respected.

Being a patriarchal society, polygamy was common in the old days especially among the ruling class, but is no longer so. Although a man may have two or more wives, the first wife is always given due respect and importance. Untouchability is unknown, although slavery existed till independence. They are a close-knit society with emphasis on community spirit. The

Khamtis are far more advanced in literature, arts, culture and civilization than most tribes of the Northeast.

They are skilled craftsmen, working in wood, ivory, gold, silver and iron. Antique shields, made of buffalo and rhinoceros hide were ornamented with gold and lac, while the 'nap' and 'pha' (swords) had carved ivory hilts. Women are still experts at weaving and embroidery.

Khamti men once sported long hair tied in a topknot. They carry their machete or *mit* in its sheath slung across their shoulders. It is always worn in the front so that the hilt is readily grasped in the right hand.

Typical Khamti houses are made of timber or bamboo on raised platforms several feet above the ground, with a notched tree trunk serving as ladder. The roofs are thatched with either palm leaves or straw, while livestock like cows and buffaloes are kept in the stockade below.

Interestingly, rice hats were used in the old days when wars were fought relentlessly and there was danger of being attacked without warning. *Khowpuk* or rice cakes made of glutinous rice, salt and powdered sesame were fashioned into hats and left to dry. In the event of any emergency, these hats were quickly worn before the person left home. If he had to spend days in the jungle in hiding, he just had to slice off a portion of his hat and eat it either raw or smoked. These innovative hats also came in handy when men set out on elephants, to look for purebred Khamti brides from places as far as Khamti Long and Yunnan in China. *Khowpuk* is still eaten today but nobody makes hats out of them any longer.

Although devout Buddhists, Khamtis by and large are non-vegetarians and enjoy their fish and meat. However, older people voluntarily become vegetarians and retire from household duties, spending most of their time in prayer and meditation. A large part of the average Khamti man's earnings are spent on religious pursuits.

Khamti literature or *Lik Tai* includes numerous hand written manuscripts on Buddhism, *Chyatuie* or chronicles, penal code, astrology, the occult, plays etc.

The typical Khamti stories are mostly about kings and queens, princes and princesses, probably due to the fact that their history is all about one kingdom being established when the previous one crumbled. The stories in this book are a cocktail of folktales, fables and legends. Khamti stories are either written in verse form or orally passed down generations, and it is therefore natural that one story may be told in different ways by different people.

1

Lengdon's Legacy

In the beginning of time when all was water, Phra created a fish. He placed some earth on the fish's back and willed it to lay an egg. Dividing the egg into two equal halves, Phra buried one half into the earth and suspended the other half above to form the sky. From the barren earth sprouted the first tree, from which all forms of life originated. The tree produced one solitary bud, which bloomed into a flower of many hues. From this flower emerged a man and a woman, the first humans to ever set foot upon the earth. That, according to the Khamtis, is how the universe came into being.

The earth now was in need of an able ruler who could ensure peace and harmony amongst men. The first men to rule the earth were the Khunlung Khunlai kings whose reign witnessed centuries of peace and prosperity. It soon came to pass that the sole surviving heir to this illustrious line of kings was a princess who was born blind. Convinced that his daughter was nothing more than a burden and a curse, the king ordered that she be put on a bamboo raft and sent adrift down the river Nam Kiu. The doomed princess prayed for death to release her from her predicament, but destiny willed otherwise. Phra knew the world would erupt in chaos if the Khunlung Khunlai dynasty came to an end and therefore dispatched Lengdon, the Thunder God, down to earth to sow the seeds of a new dynasty.

Lengdon appeared in the form of a tiger and after having rescued the princess, became intimate with her. As a result of her union with Lengdon, the princess gave birth to four sons named Chow Sukhampha, Chow Sulungpha, Chow Sukapha and Chow Sye. Having accomplished his mission, Lengdon abandoned the princess and returned to his heavenly abode.

Worthy sons of their father, the four lads grew up fearless and strong. When the princess felt the time had come, she instructed her sons to claim the throne that was rightfully theirs. The people had long given up their princess for dead and they were therefore surprised when the four brothers presented themselves before their maternal grandfather, demanding their due share of inheritance. The repentant king received them with great warmth and gave to each one of them a special gift along with an army of soldiers and settlers.

To the eldest prince Chow Sukhampha, he gifted a *kong* and bid him a fond farewell. Chow Sukhampha and his men traversed through untrodden hills and valleys for days till they reached a place where the *kong* began to boom on its own. The prince turned his horse around to face his people and said, "This place is our home now. We shall call it Maungkong." That was how the kingdom of Maungkong or the land of the *kong* came into existence.

Lengdon appeared in the form of a tiger and after having rescued the princess, became intimate with her.

The second prince Chow Sulungpha was given a *nok yang*, which perched on his shoulder as he rode out with his men. A long march later, the *nok yang* flew off and alighted on the branches of a tree next to a serene lake. Chow Sulungpha built a beautiful palace near the lake and named the new found kingdom Maungyang after the bird.

To the third prince Chow Sukapha, the old king gave a *mit*, which when they came to a far off land, flew out of its sheath and struck the ground. Chow Sukapha took that as an omen and established a new kingdom in that land, naming it Maungmit after his *mit*.

The fourth prince Chow Sye founded Maungkhay out of the land that he had been given. Thus the four half tiger princes of the Khunlung Khunlai dynasty ruled for a long, long time bringing glory to the name of their ancestors and saving the world from chaos. Following in the footsteps of their ancestors, the descendents of the princes still have their names prefixed with Su, which in Khamti means tiger.

For a long time afterwards, if a tiger was reported dead in any Khamti village, it was quite common among the Khamtis to suspend all activities for a day to mourn their common ancestor. They also paid homage to the body of the tiger by offerings of flowers.

Phra: God, the Creator; Maung: Country; Kong: Gong; Nam Kiu: Arrawady River; Maungphe: Heaven; Nok Yang: Crane; Mit: Machete; Maungkhay: Land of the youngest brother of the Tai; Chow: Sir/Master/Mister/Father.

2

Nang Chanta Looks for a Groom

In the good old days when the Nanchows were engaged in battle, there lived a willful princess whose name was Nang Chanta. When it was deemed that she was of marriageable age, her parents arranged an extravagant event whereby a hundred and fifty eligible princes were invited to compete for her hand. The assembled princes put their talents on display for the benefit of the princess, but she was hard to impress.

Would it not be better if I were to throw my stole in the air and marry the man on whose roof it falls? she sighed. *Who knows, I may find the perfect match for myself that way.* The more she thought about it, the more convinced she became that it was the only way to find true love. She conveyed her feelings to her shocked parents. The king flew into a purple rage.

"Have you taken leave of your senses? Are these brave men not good enough for you?" he demanded to know.

The king even threatened to disown her, but it seemed to have no effect on the girl whatsoever. Word spread across the kingdom that the princess had rejected all her royal suitors and was now on the lookout for a suitable groom. People flocked to get a glimpse of the princess as she stepped out of the palace gates. Who was this princess who defied her parents to look for a husband on the streets? Only a mad person would do so!

Nang Chanta's search took her through rows and rows of mansions belonging to merchants, noblemen and ministers. Every now and then she stopped to throw her gold trimmed stole in the air and each time she did that, many hearts skipped a beat. Each house owner, young or old, wished with all his heart that the stole would rest on the roof of his home. But the stole floated tantalizingly by and landed on the ground near the feet of the princess each time.

Finally, when the princess was about to give up hope of ever finding a husband, a strong gust of wind blew and carried the stole away. It sailed through the air and disappeared from view. The princess followed the direction the stole had taken and soon enough spotted her gold trimmed stole reflecting the light of the sun. It lay on the roof of a hut that belonged to a poor woodcutter who was away at work.

Since there was no one to answer the door, she paced up and down in front of the hut waiting for the owner of the house to return. *Was he young or old? What if he were ugly? What if he already had a wife?* She mused.

It was late evening when the woodcutter returned home tired and hungry. He had been able to sell some firewood and was carrying a little sack of grain. Standing by his humble hut was a girl so beautiful and richly attired, he wondered if she were a fairy and stopped in his tracks. He was half afraid to move forward, wondering if he had come to the wrong house.

"Who are you? Where have you come from?" he stuttered.

Nang Chanta's dreams were shattered when she saw a short, stout man with peasant looks in sweaty, soiled and tattered clothes. This was not what she had bargained for. But for the headstrong princess anything was better than having to admit that she was wrong.

"My name is Nang Chanta," she said. "I am the daughter of the king and now I have chosen to live here." There was a look of utter surprise on the woodcutter's face.

"How can that be? Please go away before the king sends his soldiers after me," he pleaded with folded hands.

"I have left the palace on my own accord and my father will not come to look for me. This is my home now. I cannot leave," the princess replied. She then explained how she had thrown the stole and how it had landed on his roof, making him the chosen one.

"But I cannot afford to feed you nor can I clothe you in fine silk, least of all provide you with the comforts you are used to," the woodcutter told her.

No matter how much the woodcutter tried, he was unable to make Nang Chanta alter her decision. The poor man ultimately gave up reasoning with her and so they became man and wife. Nang Chanta now had to wake up early each morning, sweep the mud floor and fetch water from the stream. Since her husband did not even own a water pot, she had to use bamboo to fetch and store water. All the drudgery was beginning to take its toll on her.

Soon her beautiful garments became soiled and frayed. Her once soft hands became coarse and lined with cuts, the fingernails broken and filled with grime. The soles of her feet were lined with cracks for her shoes wore out and had to be discarded. Her husband had not been able to sell much firewood because the villagers were poor and fetched their own supply of firewood. With no money coming in, their stock of grain was depleted and they had to live on roots and wild ferns.

After much contemplation, Nang Chanta removed the diamond ring from her finger and gave it to her husband. "Take this and sell it," she said.

"Are you sure you want to part with this ring? It is the only piece of jewellery you have," her husband wanted to know.

"Of what use is this piece of jewellery when we have nothing to eat?" she sighed, although it pained her to part with it, for it was a gift from her parents and the only thing she had that reminded her of them. The woodcutter took the ring and went to the village market. He showed it to the shopkeepers and traders there but no one seemed willing to buy it. They all knew it was worth a lot of money although they did not know how much, and none of them had that kind of money. Unable to sell the ring, the woodcutter walked home dejected. *What sort of ring is this that no one wants? It must be worthless!* He took the ring and flung it as far as he could into the river. When Nang Chanta heard of it, she almost fainted.

"You are a fool to have thrown my expensive ring away." Nang Chanta began to sob. The woodcutter could not bear to see his wife unhappy.

"There are plenty of such stones in the jungle where I go to cut wood. I can take you there and show them to you," he said.

The princess looked disdainfully at her husband. "What do you know of precious stones? You just threw the most valuable thing we had."

"Well, I have a few of them here," the woodcutter said. He took out a small bundle hidden within the layers of the thatch and handed it to his wife. When she opened the bundle she saw precious gems that were the size of eggs.

"These must be worth a fortune," she exclaimed. "Show me the place at once. Perhaps we won't be poor any longer."

Armed with huge baskets, the two of them hurried to the place where a sack full of diamonds, rubies, emeralds and other precious stones lay half hidden inside the hollow of a tree. As they scooped out the gems, a gold ring with the royal seal on it caught Nang Chanta's attention.

"That ring belongs to my father," she cried, "It was stolen a long time ago along with his collection of gems. The thief must have hidden them here and somehow could not return to collect them."

"We will return this treasure to your father," the woodcutter said.

They carried the jewels home and were so excited that they could not sleep at all. They set off for the palace early next morning. It had been a long time since Nang Chanta had left her home, and she was wondering how her parents would react when they saw her and her husband. She need not have worried for the king and queen were only too happy to have her back and all was forgiven. As part of her dowry the king presented them a beautiful palace, servants and riches.

Nang: Miss/Lady

3

Yae Sengchi Esengtum

In the good old days when the Nanchows were at war, there lived a man of comfortable means who had two wives. His first wife was simple and hard working, while the second one was shrewd and lazy. They were both blessed with a daughter each. The first wife's daughter Yae Sengchi was just as hardworking as her mother, while the second wife's daughter Esengtum displayed the same mean and slothful ways of her mother.

The man was extremely partial to his young and pretty second wife. Knowing she could get away with anything, the second wife had scant regard for the first wife although it was her duty to do so. The elder wife was up before dawn each morning to begin the day's task while the younger wife slept. After having cooked the morning meal, she would be busy either at the loom or in the fields. The hard working woman would have woven an arm's length of cloth by the time the second wife stepped out to wash the sleep off her face. Sometimes she would get up only when the sun was strong and all the work was done. She would then engage herself by going from one house to another gossiping with the neighbours.

One day Yae Sengchi's father called his two wives and said, "I have a strong urge to eat *pasa* today. Go and get some fish while I collect the herbs."

The two wives set out for the village pond with their fishing baskets. The second wife ambled along laughing and gossiping with the other women and whiling away her time. The elder wife diligently dragged her fishing basket from one end of the pond to the other. Each time she took it ou of the water and shook it, she found a fish or two. By noon her basket was filled with fish.

"Come on sister, let us go home," she called out to the second wife who was sitting under a shady tree chatting away with her friends.

The second wife did not net a single fish, and her fishing basket was dry, for she had not gone into the water. Not wanting to cut a sorry figure in front of her husband, she walked up to the first wife and sweetly said, "You must be tired sister. Let me carry your basket home and you can take mine." The first wife was indeed tired and gladly exchanged her heavy basket with the second wife.

The cunning woman hurried home after telling the first wife to rest awhile. She tousled her hair and huffed and puffed while entering the house. Her husband, meanwhile, had collected the herbs and was busy whittling bamboo sticks to skewer and smoke the fish.

"Your elder wife was so busy gossiping that she had no time to go fishing," she lied. "Look at my basket. Look at all the fish I got today."

The second wife had poisoned the husband's mind against the first wife to such an extent that he was fuming with rage. He could hardly wait for her to return home. When she did, he tipped her basket and saw that it was empty. "You lazy good for nothing woman!" he shouted angrily. "I sent you to catch fish and not to gossip." He beat her with such ferocity that the poor woman fell down unconscious and succumbed to her injuries.

Nobody mourned except for poor Yae Sengchi. The second wife was remorseless but she put on a sad face for the benefit of the villagers who had come for the cremation. Many months later, Yae Sengchi's mother came back in the form of a golden tortoise named Nang Tao Kham and lived in the lotus pond not far from her home.

With the elder wife gone, the second wife began ill treating

Yae Sengchi. She treated her like a slave and gave her scraps of leftover food to eat. While it was Yae Sengchi who did all the work, Esengtum would make a great show of being busy while actually doing nothing much.

One day as the two sisters were pounding paddy into rice, Yae Sengchi's pestle began to sing, "*Tum-tum khung*! Good fortune and fine garments will soon be yours! *Tum-tum khung!*"

One day as the two sisters were pounding paddy into rice, Yae Sengchi's pestle began to sing, *"Tum-tum khung! Good fortune and fine garments will soon be yours! Tum-tum khung!"*

Esengtum's pestle too started singing, but its words were different. *"Tum-tum sak! Days of labour and hardship are in store for you! Tum-tum sak!"*

The second wife who was nearby overheard the singing pestles and was angry. "Yae Sengchi!" she shouted. "Exchange your pestle with Esengtum!" Yae Sengchi dutifully obeyed her stepmother.

Still the pestle sang, *"Tum-tum khung! Good fortune and fine garments will soon be yours! Tum-tum khung!"*

Esengtum's pestle sang *"Tum-tum sak! Days of labour and hardship are in store for you! Tum-tum sak!"*

The second wife grabbed the pestle from Yae Sengchi and hit her on the head with it. "Since the pestles think so highly of you, let them finish all the work for you!" She stalked off with Esengtum in tow.

Yae Sengchi felt dizzy from the blow to her head, but she had to pound, fan and sort all the rice on her own. After all the work was done, she sat on the banks of the lotus pond and cried her heart out. As a child her mother had often brought her to the lotus pond. She would sit on the grassy bank and watch her mother wade into the water and collect lotus stems for their meal. Her mother would sometimes pluck a beautiful lotus flower and stick it behind her ear. Those were happy days and she wept at the thought that they were gone.

"Do not weep my daughter," she heard her mother's voice comforting her. Surprised, she looked around and saw a golden tortoise emerging from the water.

"You have nothing to fear. It is me, your dear mother who has taken this form so that I may be close to you," Nang Tao Kham said. The tortoise came up to Yae Sengchi and placed its head on her lap. Yae Sengchi hugged the tortoise and felt much better.

After that, whenever Yae Sengchi had any spare time off, she would dash off to the pond to speak to her mother. She would keep her mother informed of all the things that took place at home and in the village. It hardly mattered anymore that her stepmother severly rationed her food by giving her scraps to eat. Nang Tao Kham would purge out the most delicious food for Yae Sengchi, who would eat to her heart's content. One day Nang Tao Kham presented her daughter with a beautiful set of silk garments.

"Wear it to your cousin's marriage today," her mother said. "I know you have nothing nice to wear."

Yae Sengchi took the clothes home and wore them to her cousin's wedding. Her stepmother and Esengtum had already left for the wedding so they did not see her in her new clothes. At the wedding, people commented on how beautiful Yae Sengchi looked and gathered around to admire the intricate patterns on her garments. The stepmother being an inquisitive woman went to see what the fuss was all about. When she saw Yae Sengchi in her new clothes, she flew into a jealous rage and could barely wait to get home and confront her stepdaughter.

"Where did you get these clothes from? Did you steal my silver to buy them? Or did your lover give them to you? Speak up!" she demanded, pulling and tearing at the clothes.

Yae Sengchi remained silent, not wanting to give her secret away. This only infuriated her stepmother further. She pulled Yae Sengchi's hair and beat her so severely that she was forced to confess. "Nang Tao Kham gave them to me," she sobbed.

"Who is this Nang Tao Kham? There is no one by that name in our village," her stepmother wanted to know.

"A tortoise who lives in the lotus pond," Yae Sengchi replied.

"Why should a tortoise give you expensive clothes?" the stepmother taunted. "Who is she to you?"

Yae Sengchi did not answer.

The stepmother thought it over and came to the conclusion that it could be none other than the first wife who had come back in the form of a tortoise. She now had to find a way to get rid of the golden tortoise and so she plotted and planned till her scheming mind came up with a solution.

The wicked woman bribed Chow Ya, the local medicine man, to help her capture the golden tortoise. They both came up with a plan. She spread pieces of broken clay under her mattress and lay down on it pretending to be very ill. When her husband came home she tossed and turned about in bed, causing the pieces of clay under her mattress to crackle and break noisily. Hearing her moaning and groaning, the worried husband hurried to her bedside.

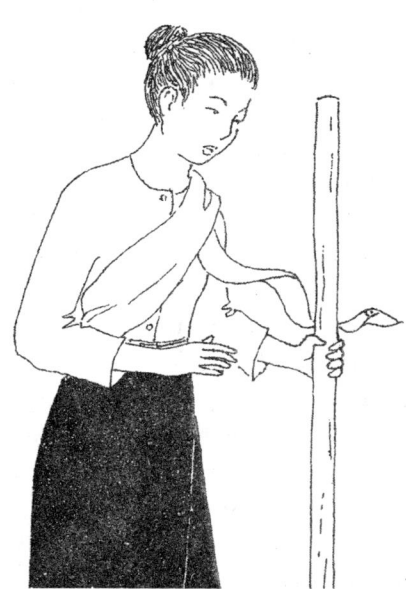

"Oh, what pain! My poor bones are breaking," she groaned. "If only Chow Ya were here to cure me." Her husband was quick to react. He took Yae Sengchi aside.

"Quick! Your mother moans in pain," he said. "Run and fetch Chow Ya at once." Chow Ya came well prepared with his odds and ends carefully tucked in his bag. Holding a bowl of water in his hand, he proceeded to chant a magic spell, as he looked the patient over.

Turning to the husband he said, "She needs to eat the flesh of the golden tortoise that lives in the lotus pond. Only then will she recover! Other than that, I see no hope at all."

The doting husband thanked Chow Ya profusely and paid him a handsome amount of money for his trouble. He immediately sent word out to all the villagers that he would reward the person who got him the golden tortoise from the lotus pond. "I must have it for my wife," he said. "If she does not eat the flesh of the tortoise she will surely die." Yae Sengchi ran to the lotus pond to warn her mother. She carried her fishing basket along and told her mother to hide in it.

All the villagers took their fishing baskets and went to the pond in a bid to catch the tortoise. They searched high and low but no one was able to catch the tortoise, let alone get a glimpse of it. All except Yae Sengchi. The tortoise hid in her fishing basket and each time Yae Sengchi lifted her basket a little she found Nang Tao Kham inside. Yae Sengchi would quickly lower her basket into the water and after a while she kept her basket in the water without lifting it. Some of the villagers grew suspicious and forced her to lift her basket out of the water. They found the tortoise hiding inside and took it to her father.

"Please do not kill it," Yae Sengchi pleaded. "It has done us no harm."

"Why? Is the tortoise more important to you than your mother? You foolish girl," her father scolded her. "Now go and fetch the firewood."

The stepmother who overheard the conversation from her bed was very pleased with the turn of events. She got out of bed and came to the kitchen to personally supervise the cooking. Both husband and wife lifted Nang Tao Kham and threw her into an iron pot and ordered Yae Sengchi to light the fire. Amid tears and futile protests, the poor girl reluctantly obeyed. As the water in the pot began to steam, Nang Tao Kham cried out, "Help! My ankles are on fire."

Yae Sengchi quickly pulled the burning log from the fire but her stepmother forced her to push it back.

"Take me out, my belly is on fire," Nang Tao Kham cried out as the fire rose higher and the water in the pot began to bubble. Yae Sengchi again tried to pull the burning log out but her stepmother immediately forced her to put it back.

"Have mercy, the heat has reached my heart," the tortoise cried faintly for the last time and died.

The water bubbled and boiled and the tortoise was cooked and served. The second wife, her husband and Esengtum ate the meat with great relish. Yae Sengchi did not eat any food that day. She cried and cried till her tears dried up.

Now that the tortoise was dead, the second wife announced that she was feeling much better. She secretly got rid of all the broken bits of clay from under her mattress and dusted her bed. In the days that followed, Yae Sengchi was made to toil all day long under her stepmother's critical supervision. Whenever her stepmother went out to visit her friends, she would go to the lotus pond hoping that her mother would make an appearance but it was all in vain.

"Mother! Mother! Where are you?" Yae Sengchi called out from the grassy bank. There was no reply.

She lifted the lotus leaves one by one. "Little fishes, have you seen my dear mother? Have you seen Nang Tao Kham?" The fishes darted out of sight for they had not forgotten the day the entire village turned their calm and quiet lotus pond into a muddy hell searching for Nang Tao Kham.

"If you happen to see Nang Tao Kham, tell her I shall come again tomorrow," Yae Sengchi told the fishes.

Then one day, a prince came riding by and saw Yae Sengchi sitting on the bank of the lotus pond. He was so enamoured by her grace and beauty that he got off his horse and went to talk to her. Yae Sengchi welcomed the chance to have someone to talk to now that her mother was no more. The sun had gone down when Yae Sengchi realized it was time she went home.

As soon as Yae Sengchi stepped into the house her angry stepmother whipped her with a cane, forbidding her to go out again without permission. When the prince failed to see Yae Sengchi at the lotus pond the following day, he made enquiries in the village and found out her name and where she lived.

The prince lost no time in reaching Yae Sengchi's house. Seeing that her guest was of noble birth, the stepmother welcomed him with open arms. The prince explained that he had come with a marriage proposal for Yae Sengchi to which the stepmother said, "Yae Sengchi is not a good match for you, your majesty. It is our Esengtum who has the qualities of a princess." She extolled the virtues of her daughter Esengtum and pressed upon the prince to accept her as a bride, but the prince was firm.

"I am here for Yae Sengchi and not her sister," he said.

Seeing that there was little she could do, the greedy stepmother demanded a large amount of gold and silver as bride price from the prince before she gave her approval. Having married the prince, Yae Sengchi was at last free of her stepmother's cruelty. Her husband's kind and considerate nature made Yae Sengchi consider herself very fortunate and blessed. Inspite of having scores of servants to wait on her, Yae Sengchi personally looked after her husband's comforts. She also took an interest in the welfare of the ordinary people and won their hearts.

In her new found happiness, Yae Sengchi forgot the ill treatment she had been subjected to by her cruel stepmother. Time and distance made her remember only the good days and forget the bad. Three years had passed when one day she expressed her desire to go and visit her parents and step sister. Her husband was a bit doubtful but seeing that his wife was so eager to go, he readily made arrangements for the journey.

When Yae Sengchi arrived at her parent's home she was warmly received and was wrongly led to believe that all was well. That night the stepmother poisoned her and after making sure that the poor girl was dead, buried her in the garden.

The following day the stepmother dressed Esengtum in her sister's garments and jewelry and sent her to the palace with strict instructions to keep herself veiled at all times. She tutored her daughter on what to say and do so as to fool the prince. The prince was surprised to find his wife back so soon and wondered why her face was covered. When he demanded an explanation she told him that a fortune teller had advised her to veil herself for a year or bad luck would befall them.

As the days passed, the prince noticed that his wife did not take any interest in tending to his needs and comforts. She preferred to laze around the whole day ordering the servants about. Her behaviour was in total contrast to that of Yae Sengchi. He could bear it no longer and decided to find out for himself. He pulled the veil off.

"What is the meaning of this?" He demanded, surprised upon seeing Esengtum instead of his beloved wife. "Where is Yae Sengchi?"

"Yae Sengchi had gone away so mother made me take her place," Esengtum replied.

"What has your wicked mother done to my wife?" the prince demanded.

Esengtum had no answer to that. She could see that the prince was very, very angry and became fearful. The prince put two and two together and came to the conclusion that the stepmother had killed Yae Sengchi so that her daughter Esengtum could replace her. Burning with anger, he called for the executioner and had Esengtum put to death. He then ordered that her body be put into a basket and sent to her parents.

When the royal guard came with the basket, the stepmother invited him in and called her husband, "We have a visitor from the palace bearing a gift. Let us see what our son-in-law has sent us."

Both husband and wife were eager to see what the basket contained. They excitedly pulled the cover off and their hearts froze upon seeing their lifeless daughter. The shock was too much for them. The husband fell down in a swoon and died, while the wife went mad with grief.

Pasa: Fish soup; Tao Kham: Golden tortoise; Tum-tum: Pound; Sak: Pestle; Khung: Garments

4

Ai Khan

Ai Khan loved nothing better than to laze all day under a shady tree, eating the discarded food offerings from the nearby temple and the over ripe fruit that fell down from the tree. He could not be bothered to work for a living. At night and on rainy days he sheltered in a cave on a little hillock on the outskirts of the city.

The people of the kingdom were terrorized by a man eating Phephai that had strayed from its own land. From snatching unsuspecting people in lonely areas, the Phephai began showing up in small villages and towns. The situation became so bad that the people decided to overcome their fears and get rid of the Phephai for good. They formed groups and kept a look out for him, chasing him with spears, arrows and swords if he did happen to show up. During an encounter, the Phephai was injured and in the confusion forgot to use his magic. While trying to flee he spied a cave and ran towards it for cover. It happened to be Ai Khan's cave. Ai Khan was lying down at the mouth of the cave enjoying the cool breeze.

"Please help me," the Phephai begged. "A mob is after my life. Save me from them and I promise to give you anything you ask for."

"Go on inside. I don't feel like moving," Ai Khan replied. The Phephai needed no further invitation. He stepped over Ai Khan and went into hiding deep within the cave.

Soon a large group of men armed with weapons approached

Ai Khan's cave. "Have you seen a Phephai pass this way?" they asked.

"I did not see anything or anyone," Ai Khan replied without bothering to get up from his comfortable position. Satisfied with his reply, the men left to search elsewhere. Long after the men had disappeared from view, Ai Khan called out to the Phephai, "You can come out now, there's no one here but me."

The Phephai was extremely grateful. "What is it you want?" he asked. "Gold, diamonds or maybe a kingdom?"

Ai Khan scratched his head thoughtfully and replied, "I want none of those things. All I want is to know the language of each and every thing that can be found on earth. I desire nothing more."

The demon was surprised at Ai Khan's request, but a promise was a promise and so he gave Ai Khan the gift of understanding the language of all living and non-living things. The Phephai, however, cautioned, "If you reveal this to anyone I shall appear out of nowhere and eat you that very instant."

The Phephai went his way and Ai Khan spent his time listening to the birds, animals and trees talk. He especially loved talking to the king's horses and became so friendly with them that they obeyed his every command. The king was very impressed with Ai Khan and appointed him as the head of the royal stables. The king had three sons whom Ai Khan accompanied on their frequent travels.

One day while travelling abroad, they pitched camp on the banks of a river and killed a wild boar. As they sat down to roast the meat, five comely maidens carrying waterpots came along. Without uttering a single word the five girls poured water over the fire, thereby putting it off.

When the princes protested, the girls tossed their heads arrogantly and said, "Our father is the king of this land and you have not taken our permission to camp here."

"Well, in that case may we take your permission now?" the eldest prince asked.

"Only on one condition. We challenge you to a plate fight.

Bring all the plates that you want but they should only be made of China. Meet us at the royal stadium on the seventh day," the eldest princess said. The challenge was accepted.

The princesses sent messengers to all parts of the kingdom to tell people not to sell plates to any strangers. Those who did would be severely punished. Under these circumstances, the three princes were unable to buy a single plate within that kingdom. They were at a loss, for without plates they could not take up the challenge and if they did not show up, they would be labelled cowards. They were so worried that they went hungry for two days.

Seeing the predicament the princes were in, Ai Khan went up to them and said, "Don't worry masters. I know a way out. Just trust me and give me some money to buy a horse so that I can go home and get some plates." The princes gave him the money for they were desperate enough to try anything.

Ai Khan went to a horse trader with the largest stables in the city and was shown the best horses. He walked from one end of the stable to the other, inspecting each and every horse, until he came to the last one in the corner. It was the thinnest, ugliest horse he had ever seen. Its coat was dull and it looked like it had not eaten in days.

"Don't they give you any food? You certainly look funny," Ai Khan said to the horse.

"Looks are deceptive," replied the horse. "If my owner knew my capabilities he would treat me better."

"What are you capable of doing that other horses can't?" asked Ai Khan.

"I can fly and reach any destination in an instant," the horse replied. "An ordinary horse would take three months to travel the distance I could cover in a blink."

"So what are you doing here?" asked Ai Khan. "What's stopping you from flying away."

"I am too weak at the moment. If you take me with you and look after me well, I will take you anywhere you wish," the horse said. Ai Khan went to the horse trader and told him he wanted to buy the thin horse.

"Are you crazy? I have the best horses and yet you prefer that skinny one?" the man asked. Seeing that Ai khan was determined to take the thin horse, the trader sold it to him at a good bargain.

When the princes saw the horse they were dismayed. "Have you gone mad?" the eldest prince remarked. "What do you hope to achieve with this?"

"Be patient master," Ai Khan replied. "This animal is our only hope."

For the next three days Ai Khan diligently fed and watered the horse. He clipped its tail, bathed and brushed it till its coat took on a shine. At the end of the third day, the horse looked well groomed and healthy.

"I am ready to take you wherever you wish to go, master," the horse told him. Ai Khan mounted the horse and told it to take him back to his kingdom. The very next moment he found himself at the palace gates. He met the king and informed him about the whereabouts of his sons and the problems they were facing. The king told Ai Khan to check the royal store and take as many plates as he needed.

Ai Khan walked into the store. There was a huge cupboard, the shelves of which were stacked with the best china. He went to the cupboard and gave it a sound kick. The plates tinkled and wobbled about. One of them shouted, "I can defeat ten thousand plates." Ai khan removed the plate from the shelf and put it in his bag.

Another plate shouted, "That's nothing! I can defeat a hundred thousand plates." Ai Khan promptly took that one too.

Yet another plate shouted, "I'm the best! I can defeat a thousand times more than a hundred thousand plates." Ai Khan took the third plate and rushed back to the princes. Their faces fell when they saw that Ai Khan had only three plates with him.

"Don't worry masters. Leave it to me," Ai Khan told them. They had no option but to leave it all to Ai Khan. Armed with their three plates, they went to the stadium at the appointed time and were shown their seats. The princesses sat on the opposite side. Behind them were cartloads of plates of all shapes and sizes. The princesses laughed when they saw that the princes carried only one plate each.

When the gong was sounded to announce the commencement of the big fight, the eldest prince held up his plate and hit it against the plate of the first princess. Hers broke. He hit the second plate. That broke too. The second princess came forward but could not fare better. The next came, and the next and the next until ten thousand plates lay scattered in pieces on the ground. The prince's plate finally cracked. It was now time for the second prince to come forward. His plate broke after smashing a hundred thousand plates. Finally the third prince took up the challenge and went on smashing plate after plate till there were no more plates left in the entire kingdom. The princesses had to admit defeat amidst the mounds of broken china.

The king who had watched the contest was greatly impressed by the three princes and offered them his daughters in marriage. The eldest was married off to Ai Khan. Each princess was given a portion of the kingdom as dowry. Ai Khan now lived in a luxurious palace and his horse was kept in a roomy stable. He also kept a cat and a dog as pets.

* * *

One day while Ai Khan and his wife were having their meal, the cat and dog were arguing loudly outside.

"My master loves me more because he lets me sleep on the bed while you are made to sleep outside," the cat purred.

"He loves me more because he takes me everywhere he goes and leaves you home," the dog growled back.

"If that is so, then why do I get all the fish and meat while you only get the bones?" the cat mewed.

Finding the whole conversation amusing, Ai Khan could not

suppress his laughter. The surprised wife took offence for she was certain her husband was laughing at her expense. She demanded an explanation.

Ai Khan could not tell her why because of his promise to the Phephai. On the other hand his wife would be annoyed if he did not tell her. He was in a dilemma. He told his wife, "I cannot tell you the real reason because if I do, we cannot remain together." His wife was all the more curious and not being one to give up so easily she kept on insisting till he told her to follow him to the stable if she wanted to know the truth. He mounted his horse and held a whip in his hand.

Looking down at his bewildered wife, Ai Khan said, "Believe me, I was not laughing at you. I was merely laughing over what the cat and dog were arguing about. No one knows it but I can actually understand the animal language."

As soon as he had finished his sentence, he heard the Phephai's thunderous laugh. "You have broken your promise and I have come to keep mine!"

Ai Khan whipped his horse and the animal flew off at lightening speed with the Phephai in hot pursuit. They flew over mountains, valleys and rivers until they saw the sea in front of them. The Phephai could not cross the sea. He thumped his chest in frustration until he fell down dead. The horse flew over the entire length of the sea and collapsed exhausted on the beach at the other end. Try as he might, Ai Khan could not revive his horse.

With his horse now dead, Ai Khan roamed aimlessly on the deserted beach for days until he spotted a passing ship. Ai Khan shouted as loud as he could, waving his arms about, trying to draw the attention of the sailors. As luck would have it, someone on board saw him and the ship dropped anchor to pick him up.

The ship belonged to a merchant who allowed Ai Khan to sail with them as helper. Days turned into weeks and months till Ai Khan wondered if he would spend the rest of his life on the seas. He often thought of his wife and what she must be doing. One day as Ai Khan was strolling on the deck he heard voices from above. Looking up he saw two large gems atop the mast. Both of them were arguing with one another as to which one of them was better.

"I can bring the dead back to life," one of them boasted. The other one retorted, "I can do better. If someone puts me in his mouth I can take him wherever he wishes to go."

That night when everyone was asleep, Ai Khan climbed up and quietly removed the two stones. He put the transporter stone in his mouth and wished himself back to the spot where his horse lay. No sooner had he made his wish then he found himself next to his horse. He rubbed the inert horse with the life giving stone and lo and behold! It came back to life. With both stones safely in his pocket, Ai Khan mounted his faithful horse and flew homeward.

On the way Ai Khan saw the Phephai lying dead on the beach. *I wonder if the stone is powerful enough to bring him back to life*, he thought to himself and alighted next to the Phephai. He rubbed the stone against the Phephai's chest and to his surprise the Phephai came back to life. The Phephai had been dead for a long time and was extremely hungry. It stretched out its hand to catch hold of Ai Khan.

"Ungrateful wretch!" shouted Ai Khan, "I bring you back to life and you still want to eat me? Don't you realize if I can bring you back to life I can also kill you again?" The Phephai realized his folly and begged forgiveness. He quickly disappeared and was never heard of again.

Ai Khan flew back home to his wife, who had given him up for dead. He showed his wife the magic stones and related his adventures.

"With these stones in our possession, we could live forever and go wherever our fancy takes us," Ai Khan told his wife. They travelled to all corners of the earth and grew wrinkled with age but because of the stone that gave them eternal life they lived on and on.

One day Ai Khan passed a comment, which he thought his

wife would find amusing. "You have more lines on your face than the number of hairs on your head," he told her.

Far from being amused she was angry and hurt at her husband for speaking to her in such a manner. She took the two stones and threw them into the sea. As soon as she did that, both husband and wife fell down dead. Their bodies turned into dust and were scattered by the wind. As for the two stones, they lie at the bottom of the sea.

Phephai: Demon, Ogre; Khan: Lazy

5

Nang Pham & the Three Suitors

Nang Pham was a shrewd and opportunistic girl who lived in a ramshackle house all by herself. There were three young men from a nearby village who tried to woo her. Nang Pham encouraged all three of them and used her wiles to get the young men to run errands for her.

Tam Leng visited her in the mornings and would fetch the water from the river and tend to her vegetable garden. Hokham would appear in the afternoons and chop the firewood for her. Kangkhun would come at night and keep watch while she slept. Nang Pham spoke sweetly to all three of them and sent them on their way before it was time for the other to arrive. This comfortable arrangement continued for a while. One day she noticed that her verandah was on the verge of collapse and in urgent need of repairs. When she asked her three suitors to get the bamboo required for the job, they were more than eager to oblige.

"While you are in the jungle cutting the bamboo, I shall cook you a delicious meal of chicken and rice. Start at daybreak and when you have cut ten poles you can come and collect your lunch," she told Tam Leng.

To Hokham she said, "Start at daybreak and after you have cut fifteen poles you can come and collect your lunch."

Kangkhun was instructed to collect his lunch after he had cut twenty poles. In this way none of them would know anything about the other.

The next morning Nang Pham began preparing lunch for the three men. She cooked chicken in bamboo shoot gravy and divided it neatly into three portions, which she then wrapped in leaves. Wrapping a ball of rice for each one of her suitors, she sat down and waited for the young men to collect their meal.

Tam Leng, Hokham and Kangkhun started off at daybreak and met at the forest. Quite by chance they had all decided to cut bamboo from the same grove. They exchanged polite conversation and went about their work. Tam Leng left the grove after he had cut ten poles, collected his lunch and resumed his work. Hokham went for his lunch after cutting fifteen poles and Kangkhun went only after he had cut twenty poles. Since they all came at different times, none of them met at Nang Pham's house.

It was high noon when the three men decided to sit down and share their meal. Tam Leng opened his leaf and the aroma of the bamboo shoot assailed his nostrils. "My girl friend has given me a chicken leg in bamboo shoot gravy," he declared proudly. "No one can cook as well as her."

"Mine too has given me a dish similar to yours," Hokham said. "Chicken leg in bamboo shoot gravy."

"How strange! Mine too is chicken in bamboo shoot gravy, but minus the leg portion," exclaimed Kangkhun.

"Let us see if this leg belongs to your chicken," Tam Leng said jokingly, picking up his piece of chicken leg and placing it next to Kangkhun's piece. Hokham did the same thing with his piece. All the three pieces fit perfectly. It really was one bird divided into three portions! They looked incredulously at the chicken and then at each other.

"What is your girlfriend's name?" Tam Leng asked the other two.

"Nang Pham!" They replied.

They also discovered that they were all cutting bamboo for the same girl without knowing it. Slowly it dawned on them that Nang Pham had only been using them for her own selfish reasons. Realizing that they had been made fools of, the three men decided to confront Nang Pham.

"Let's teach her a lesson," Hokham said. They all went to Nang Pham's house and forcibly took her with them. They decided to sell her off at the slave market in the city and took turns carrying her on their backs. Nang Pham was no lightweight and before long the young men were exhausted from carrying their heavy burden. They sat down under the shade of a tree near a paddy field to regain their strength, but the warm sun and cool breeze soon put the three tired men to sleep. The owner of the paddy field happened to be inspecting his crop. Seeing the three sleeping men and the girl, the man went forward and asked the girl what they were doing there.

Nang Pham was no lightweight and before long the young men were exhausted from carrying their heavy burden.

"I am on my way to the city to sell these slaves," she said, pointing to the sleeping men.

"Well, I do need some workers so you can sell them to me," the man said. They settled at a price and after the money exchanged hands, Nang Pham made a quick getaway.

The owner of the field picked up a stick and prodded the three sleeping men with it. "Time to get up and work. I didn't pay to watch you sleep all day!"

Tam Leng, Hokham and Kangkhun woke up with a start. Rubbing the sleep off their eyes, they looked around and saw that Nang Pham was nowhere in sight. Instead there was this fat man poking them with a stick, telling them to go to work. They drew their swords and chased the startled man away.

"She has tricked us again. This time we won't spare her. We must finish her off for good!" Kangkhun declared angrily.

Meanwhile, Nang Pham had reached home and was plotting to get rid of all three men. Knowing they would come back for her sooner or later, she prepared food and drinks mixed with a poisonous herb and waited. When they barged in through her door she very sweetly exclaimed, "I was expecting you all to come, so I've prepared some food and drinks. Come, let us eat first and then discuss what we have to do."

Having walked all the way in the hot sun, the three men were tired, hungry and thirsty. The aroma of the food was too tempting to resist and the three men ate and drank to their heart's content. The poison took effect and soon after they were all dead. Nang Pham lost no time in planning her next move. She hid two of the dead men inside and dragged Tam Leng's body out on the verandah. Sitting next to his body she waited for someone to pass by. Sure enough Konmuk, a foolish man, was walking along the road. Nang Pham let out a loud wail that soon had Konmuk running towards her house.

"Why are you crying sister?" he asked in a concerned manner.

"I've lost my dear husband and I cannot even carry him to his grave," she sobbed. Konmuk thought it was an opportunity for him to earn some quick money.

"I'll bury him for you if you will pay me for it," Konmuk said.

"I'll pay you whatever you ask," Nang Pham replied.

Konmuk carried Tam Leng's body and buried him a little way off near the forest. In the meantime Nang Pham brought out Hokham's body and went down to dirty her feet in the wet mud. She walked up the steps with muddy feet leaving her footprints all over the steps and the verandah.

When Konmuk came back to collect his payment, she pointed to the muddy footprints near the body and wept, "You must have buried him in a shallow grave. That's why he has walked back home." Konmuk looked at the muddy footprints and believed her.

"What should we do now?" Konmuk asked her.

"I think you should take him and throw him into the river," Nang Pham suggested. "The current will carry him downstream and he won't be able to walk back."

Konmuk picked up the body and made his way down towards the river. As soon as Konmuk left with Hokham's body, she quickly brought out Kangkhun's body and splashed it with a pot full of water. When Konmuk returned after throwing the body into the river, he was amazed to see that there was a body lying on the verandah drenched in water.

"He has come back from the river," she wailed. "This time please burn him so that he is gone for good."

Konmuk carried the body to the cremation ground and burned it. This time he made sure that the job was thorough. Totally exhausted from ferrying the bodies to their graves, Konmuk wiped his brow and started walking towards Nang Pham's house to collect his payment.

A farmer had just finished setting his fields on fire and was returning home covered with soot. Konmuk saw the farmer and ran towards him shouting, "It's you again! I buried you and you came back. I threw you into the river and you managed to come back. Now you have come back after I had just burned you."

He tried to catch hold of the farmer but the farmer thought him mad and pushed him away. Konmuk would have none of it. He wasn't about to let go of this man who kept coming back from the grave. After all, he had to collect his money for the three times that he had gone about disposing off the body. The two of them grappled with each other and soon a curious crowd gathered around to watch them.

"Why are the two of you fighting?" someone from the crowd asked after they were forcibly separated.

"He's not a man but a ghost. He keeps coming back from the grave," Konmuk pointed his finger at the farmer.

"He's a mad man I tell you!" the farmer shouted back. There were a few people who knew the farmer and they demanded an explanation from Konmuk.

Konmuk related the events of the day and led them all to Nang Pham's house. Nang Pham pretended she did not know Konmuk. "I have never seen him before," she lied. Konmuk then led them to Tam Leng's grave. Realizing she was cornered, Nang Pham tried to escape but was caught and brought before the village council. After she was pronounced guilty of murder, the angry villagers put her in a bamboo basket and threw her into the fast flowing river.

6

Wo Pem Samlo

In a little village on the banks of a mighty river, there lived a farmer, his wife and five daughters. They were a happy family until one day, the river flooded its banks and swallowed the village. The farmer's wife and four daughters were washed away by the floods leaving the farmer and his youngest daughter Wo Pem the only survivors in the family. The farmer later married a beautiful but wicked woman who had no intention of playing mother to someone else's child except her own daughter Oak Pin.

Wo Pem and Oak Pin were two very different individuals. Oak Pin was very quick but her work was slipshod. She was selfish and demanding, always bullying Wo Pem and making fun of her. Wo Pem on the other hand was a good-natured girl who did her work slowly and diligently. As a result she was labelled a slow coach and a dullard, while her younger sister was praised for her efficiency.

Wo Pem's father was growing old and his failing health did not permit him to plough the fields any more.

"I think it is time we got our children married and let our sons-in-law help us with our work," he said to his wife.

Let us get our daughter Oak Pin married off to Samlo," the stepmother suggested. "He has no parents and is very hard working. He can live here with us."

Wo Pem's father went to Samlo's house and spoke to his uncle. "We would like Samlo as a son-in-law and have him live with us," he said.

"It is for Samlo to decide," the uncle answered. Samlo willingly agreed to the proposal for he thought Wo Pem would make a good wife.

Wo Pem's father went home and happily related everything to his wife. Instead of being happy, she was furious, for Samlo had chosen Wo Pem and not her daughter. Samlo proved to be a very good husband. Both husband and wife enjoyed working together. Samlo would do the heavy work, leaving the lighter work for Wo Pem. He was also an ideal son-in-law, shouldering all the responsibility and spending time talking to his in-laws.

The stepmother could not bear to see the two of them together. Her feelings towards Wo Pem grew more bitter by the day. "If only I could get rid of her," she thought. "Why should Wo Pem be happy when my poor daughter still remains unmarried?"

"Samlo is nothing but his wife's servant," Oak Pin would say unkindly for Wo Pem to hear. No decent man in the village wanted to marry Oak Pin because of her quarrelsome nature. Matters worsened when Wo Pem was expecting her first child. Samlo was even more attentive to his wife and this only infuriated the stepmother further.

The jealous woman would scold her for no reason whatsoever, telling her what a slow and useless person she was. Samlo had no idea that Wo Pem was ill treated and disliked by her stepmother, for the cunning woman was double faced. In front of her son-in-law she was all sugar and honey but the moment his back was turned she showed her true colours. Wo Pem suffered in silence for she did not want to burden Samlo with her problems. The stepmother's evil mind worked overtime, trying to think of ways to get rid of Wo Pem without arousing anyone's suspicion. At last she thought she had the perfect plan. She took a long strip of cane and whittled one side of it till it was as sharp as a blade. She rolled it and hid it among her baskets so that no one saw it.

One day when Samlo had gone fishing, the stepmother sent Wo Pem to the river to fetch water. While Wo Pem was filling the waterpot, her stepmother quickly tied the strip of cane to the handrail, keeping the sharpened edge upward. After her evil deed was done, she went to her room and shut the door. Wo Pem returned home from the river with a pot of water resting on her hip and the crook of her arm.

While climbing up the steps she ran her palm over the handrail and cried out in pain as the cane sliced through her fingers and blood gushed freely from the gaping wound. The poor girl lost her balance and tumbled down, her water pot on one side of the steps and she on the other. Her piteous cries were enough to bring the neighbours running, but not her stepmother. The woman emerged from her room pretending surprise and shock only after she heard the neighbours exclaim that Wo Pem was dead.

When Samlo returned home later that evening and saw his beloved wife lying in a bloodied shroud, he wept in anguish. Unable to cope with the sudden loss, Samlo took his own life so that he could join her in the spirit world. Neighbours carried their bodies to the riverside and buried them next to each other. The stepmother could not understand why Samlo had taken his own life. She blamed Wo Pem for his death and to punish the poor girl erected a bamboo fence separating the two graves from one another.

Wo Pem and Samlo came back as stars, with Samlo being the larger of the two. If you look at the heavens you will see two bright stars coming close to each other. Just as they are about to touch one another, they slowly move further and further apart. Wo Pem and Samlo can never be united even as stars because of the fence that separates them.

7

The Milky Way

A very long time ago, there lived a beautiful girl by the name of Nang Sanleng. Her father being a rich merchant would go on long journeys and bring her expensive gifts from far off shores. Each time before he left on his journeys he would ask his daughter if there was anything she wanted. On one such occassion she asked him to bring her a talking bird.

He travelled far and wide looking for a bird that could talk but could not find any. Not wanting to disappoint his child, he continued his search although he had long finished all the work he had set out to do. He finally visited a country where talking birds were available and paid a large sum of money for a female mynah.

Nang Sanleng was very happy and began teaching it to speak in Khamti. Her father called the goldsmith and had a special golden cage made for the bird. The cage hung in the courtyard near a lily pond just outside her room. Nang Sanleng spent long happy hours talking to the mynah and fed and watered it herself, not trusting her servants to take care of it. She was careful to lock the door of the cage and keep the golden key in her person, lest it fly away.

Nang Sanleng loved going for a stroll along the riverbank not far from her house. The current was very swift especially towards the other side, preventing anyone in the village from venturing too far out on their boats.

Then one day, as Nang Sanleng took her usual walk along

Nang Sanleng was very happy and began teaching it to speak in Khamti.

the riverbank, she saw something or rather someone riding the waves. It seemed to be heading towards her. That someone turned out to be a handsome youth on a monstrous crocodile. *He must be a magician from a far off island,* she thought. *Who else could cross the waves and reach this far?*

The youth dismounted and approached her. "My name is Chow Shwetakung," he said by way of introduction. "I live across the river."

Nang Sanleng was flattered by the look of admiration in the handsome stranger's eyes. They made small talk, unmindful of the time until darkness shrouded them.

Nang Sanleng became aware of the lateness of the hour and exclaimed, "I must take your leave or my mother will come looking for me."

Chow Shwetakung reluctantly took his leave, but not before both promised to meet again the following day. He walked to the river and slapped the water three times with his magic cane. The waters churned and from its swirling depths emerged his reptilian mount. Chow Shwetakung leapt upon the crocodile, waved to her and disappeared from view. Nang Sanleng went home flushed with happiness and dreamed of the handsome young man she had just met.

True to his word, Chow Shwetakung was waiting for Nang Sanleng by the river the next day. From then onward they met every single day and soon their friendship blossomed into love. Nang Sanleng could not keep her love a secret for long. She confided in her childhood friend. The friend in turn became impatient to have a glimpse of the mysterious stranger who had cast a spell on Nang Sanleng.

"Will your parents agree to let you marry a stranger from an unknown land?" the friend was curious to know.

"My parents have never refused me anything," Nang Sanleng replied confidently.

"What about his parents?" the friend asked. "Will they send a proposal for you?"

Nang Sanleng was taken aback for she did not even know anything about his family. *What if his parents decided against the marriage?*

"Please go and meet him," she told her friend. "Find out from him whether he is serious about marrying me. I must know."

When the friend set eyes on Chow Shwetakung, she fell in love with him and became extremely jealous of Nang Sanleng. She asked Chow Shwetakung, "Why do you always carry a cane?"

"I use it to summon the crocodile," Chow Shwetakung replied. "It is a special cane."

"Only a brave man like you can subdue a monster such as the one you ride on," she said in admiring tones. "How do you manage to do that?"

Chow Shwetakung was flattered. "It is because I do not let any girl lay her head on my arms. If I let that happen, I would lose my power," He confessed. This was all that the friend needed to hear. If she could not get him, neither could her friend.

Nang Sanleng was eagerly awaiting her friend's return. "What did he say?" she asked anxiously. "What have you found out? Tell me quickly!"

"He told me nothing but since you both are so in love, you must be doing what other girls do," the friend smiled mysteriously.

"Tell me! What is it that other girls do? Nang Sanleng was curious to know.

"Oh, they use their boyfriend's arms to rest their head on, just like they would use a pillow," the friend replied. She then suggested that Nang Sanleng do the same to find out whether Chow Shwetakung's love for her was true.

The very next day when the two lovers met, she said, "If you truly love me, allow me to rest my head on your arms." Chow Shwetakung was taken aback.

"Ask me for anything else but that," he retorted. Nang Sanleng fell into a sulk and said, "It just shows you do not love me. All lovers do it."

Chow Shwetakung tried to reason with her but Nang Sanleng would not listen. When she threatened to leave him he relented.

"If you insist, you may use my little finger as a pillow," he said in resignation. Nang Sanleng put her head on Chow Shwetakung's little finger and felt reassured.

Next day when Chow Shwetakung slapped the water with his cane the crocodile did not appear. He thrashed the waves till the cane grew limp but the crocodile was nowhere to be seen. Seeing that he had lost his powers, Chow Shwetakung threw the cane into the river in frustration and went home sad and dejected. Without the help of the crocodile, Chow Shwetakung could not cross the river. Nang Sanleng waited for him and when his absence grew longer, she began to think that he had forgotten her. She went to the riverbank every day, straining her eyes over the crashing waves but there was no sign of Chow Shwetakung. It seemed like her love had been a dream after all.

On the other side of the river, Chow Shwetakung wandered around lost in his thoughts. The mynah that nested under his roof felt sorry for him. "Why are you sad, my friend?" it asked.

"I cannot cross the river to meet my beloved. I wonder if she still thinks of me," Chow Shwetakung sighed and looked at the bird, "You can fly wherever you wish to go. Will you carry a message for me to my dear Nang Sanleng?"

The bird agreed and with Chow Shwetakung's letter in its beak, soared above the clouds and crossed the wide river to where Nang Sanleng lived. It perched on the roof of Nang Sanleng's house and called out her name, "Nang Sanleng! Nang Sanleng!"

"Who are you?" the female mynah chirped. "How do you know my mistress by her name?" Hearing her voice the male bird looked down and saw a pretty mynah inside a cage from which hung a golden lock.

"What are you doing behind those bars?" he asked, for he had never encountered a bird in a cage before.

"This is my home," the female bird replied. "I have lived here all my life."

"Oh, you poor thing! I truly pity you." The male bird said. "How do you spend your time inside your little cage? Does your mistress ever let you out?"

"My mistress is very kind. She gives me everything I need, so I need not venture out," the female bird replied.

"Well, then you know nothing about life," the male bird said. "Where is your mistress? I have a letter for her from Chow Shwetakung."

At that moment Nang Sanleng came out to feed her bird. She stopped in her tracks when she saw the male bird with an envelope in its beak. The bird dropped the letter at her feet and chirped, "Chow Shwetakung waits for a reply." Nang Sanleng excitedly tore open the envelope and read her beloved's letter. She quickly wrote back a reply and gave it to the male bird.

Chow Shwetakung was waiting impatiently for the bird to return. When he read Nang Sanleng's letter his joy knew no bounds. The letters between the two lovers flew fast and furious and the male bird was kept busy flying to and fro. It was only natural that while he waited for Nang Sanleng to write out her reply, he kept himself engaged in conversation with the female bird. They gradually fell in love with one another.

"I wish I could take you out of that cage and show you the world," the male bird said. "I really wish I could."

"What is it like outside?" she asked wonderingly. The male bird told her how big the world was. He spoke of the snow in the mountains, the emerald green of the forests and the joy of flying over fields of ripe corn and meeting others of their kind. The female bird listened in rapt attention, not being able to comprehend the sheer wonder of what he was telling her. She hopped about inside her little gold cage and twittered, "I have never flown before. Do you think I can?"

"All birds are meant to fly," the male bird said. "It would be the same for a man if his legs were chained. He would still be able to walk once the chains were removed."

The female bird poked her pretty head out through the bars and looked around as if seeing things for the first time. "Some day when my mistress forgets to lock me up, you could teach me to fly."

The male bird felt immense pity for her. At least his master did not keep him caged, but humans could not be trusted. He wanted to show his friend the world. To help her experience how wonderful it was to be free to fly wherever the heart desired. He imagined them building a nest of their own somewhere deep in the emerald forests far away from the eyes of men.

"I shall find a way to get you out, my dear," he promised before departing with Nang Sanleng's letter. That night the male bird made up its mind to put an end to the suffering of his little friend, even if it meant deception.

"Chow Shwetakung is planning to elope with Nang Sanleng," the male mynah revealed when he came again the following day.

"That means we shall all live together in your home," the female mynah said happily. She was certain that her mistress would never leave her behind. Her friend was doubtful.

"How can you be so sure? Even if she took you along, do you think your mistress will ever let you out of your cage? We can never be together unless you escape," the male bird said.

That day he did not hand over the letter to Nang Sanleng, but instead took it back. Chow Shwetakung was busy building a strong boat to take him across the river. When he saw that the bird had carried his letter back he asked, "Did you not give my letter to Nang Sanleng?"

"Nang Sanleng is no more," the mynah lied. "She is dead and gone forever."

It dropped the unopened letter to the ground and flew away. Overcome with grief, Chow Shwetakung took his own life. The mynah then flew across the river to Nang Sanleng's house to inform her about Chow Shwetakung's death.

It waited for Nang Sanleng to come out and open the door of the cage. As soon as she put her hand in to put the food inside, the male bird flew down from the branch above to perch on the top of the cage. "Chow Shwetakung is dead," it said. "He will never write again." Nang Sanleng stood rooted to the spot, the colour draining off her pretty face.

"Tell me if it's a lie," she said. "Did you see him die?" The mynah fluttered its wings and said, "I was there when he called out to you before he died. Why would I lie?"

Nang Sanleng sank to the ground in grief and never recovered. She did not hear the male bird coaxing the female mynah out of the cage. She did not see her pretty feathered friend step hesitantly out of the open door of the cage and glide unsteadily down to the ground. Together the two lovers spread their wings and soared high into the open skies.

When Nang Sanleng's parents came out into the courtyard, they found their beloved daughter stretched out on the ground, motionless. Sadly, they carried her body to the riverbank and cremated her. On the other side of the raging river, Chow Shwetakung's body was being cremated at the same time. The smoke from the two funeral pyres rose high in the air and merged as one. Their spirits were united and their love twinkled across the universe to become what is known as the Milky Way.

8

Ai Khai Ngup

Ai Khai Ngup was a foolish man who met up with two other fools like him and the three became fast friends. They did everything together and got on so well that they even decided to dress alike. Sometimes it was difficult to tell one from the other. The villagers did not take them seriously and the children called them rude names and played pranks on them. Ai Khai Ngup and his friends were fed up of being the butt of cruel jokes played by the village children and decided to leave the village for good.

"Where shall we go?" Ai Khai Ngup asked his two companions one day.

"Let's explore the world," the first fool said. "We've been in this village ever since we were born. It's time we saw something new."

"That's true!" the second fool agreed solemnly. "It's time we saw how big the world is. No one will miss us."

They bundled their few belongings and went to bid their neighbours goodbye. "Where do you think you three are going?" the village headman asked.

"We think it is time we saw the world," Ai Khai Ngup answered.

The old man narrowed his eyes and looked doubtful. "Are you sure the three of you will be able to do it?" he said. "The world is very large and none of you have ever been out before."

"That is exactly why we are doing it," the first fool said. "Goodbye, we must leave now." The three fools trudged towards the banks of the river.

Since they could not swim across the river, they decided to look for a boat. After walking some distance they came to a huge boat yard, which had an amazing collection of boats of all shapes and sizes. The three fools inspected each and every boat wondering which one would be ideally suited for them.

"Stop! Turn left!" they shouted in turn, but the water horse seemed to have a mind of its own, bobbing up and down with the rise and fall of the waves.

"This one looks nice, but it's too big for us," the first fool said.

"Look at that one there!" the second fool shouted excitedly, pointing to an elaborately carved boat. However it turned out to be unsuitable.

"Let's look for something that will take us to our destination very quickly," Ai Khai Ngup said. "Look over there! Isn't that a nice water horse?" he asked.

His two companions looked in the direction he was pointing and exclaimed, "That's just what we need!" The water horse in question was a boat with a fierce dragon carved on it. It looked impressive and sturdy and was just the kind of boat they were looking for.

"Whom does it belong to?" they asked the man who had been watching them all along.

"This is the king's boat yard and I am the keeper," the man replied in a self-important manner.

"Can we borrow that water horse?" Ai Khai Ngup asked, pointing to the boat they had decided upon.

"That's the fastest water horse we have here, but you'd better bring it back in the same condition or the king will send you to prison," he warned.

The three fools scrambled onto the boat and yelled, "Come on water horse, take us to our destination." They did not even pick up the oars, expecting the water horse to follow their commands.

The current carried the boat and its passengers downstream slowly at first, and then at an alarming speed. "Stop! Turn left!" they shouted in turn, but the water horse seemed to have a mind of its own, bobbing up and down with the rise and fall of the waves. At times it veered towards the right and at times left. It just did not go in the direction it was told to. The three fools gripped hard at the sides of the water horse, hoping it might turn in the direction they were holding on to.

"Come on water horse, turn to the right... ...the right!" the first fool urged. The three fools gripped the sides of the boat and tried to steer it to the right. The water horse of course did not listen.

"What a stupid horse this is!" exclaimed Ai Khai Ngup in disgust. He pulled out his sword and hacked both sides of the boat with all his might. "Come on friends, let's beat this stubborn water horse."

And beat it they did, till the water horse fell apart and the fools were dragged under water. They struggled to stay afloat and managed to get ashore. Wet and angry, they went straight to the boat keeper.

"What happened?" the boat keeper asked. "Where is the boat you took?"

"What a stubborn horse that was!" they said. "We cut it up because it did not listen to us. We almost drowned but we were lucky."

The boat keeper was speechless with shock. He immediately took them to the king.

"Your water horse is useless! It refuses to obey instructions and does what it pleases," Ai Khai Ngup complained.

At first the king was amused and laughed at their stupidity, but when he heard of the damage they had done to his boat, he was furious.

"Idiots!" he thundered. "That was my prized boat. Are you so ignorant you mistake a boat for a horse? Get out of my sight before I feed you to the crocodiles."

The fools hurriedly left the palace before the king changed his mind. They decided to build a new boat and gift it to the king as a token of gratitude for not having punished them. Making their way into the forest to look for some wood to build the king's boat, they saw a tall tree, which they thought was ideal for the purpose.

"We need a straight log in order to make a boat," the first fool said. "So, I'm going to find out if this one is straight." The only way to do that was to climb up the tree, he thought. When he had reached the topmost branch and was satisfied that the tree was as straight as could be, he told his companions to begin the job of cutting the tree.

Ai Khai Ngup swung his axe and started chopping the tree. The second fool stood on the opposite side with outstretched arms waiting to catch the falling tree. It took a long time before the tree fell with a mighty crash, killing the first and the second fool.

When Ai Khai Ngup saw his friends lying on the ground with their mouths open, he presumed they were grinning.

"Why are you laughing?" he asked, and when they did not reply he added, "If you want to sleep in the forest, that's your choice, but I'm leaving. I'll come back tomorrow and we can begin our work."

Next morning Ai Khai Ngup was summoned by the king who asked him the whereabouts of his companions. Ai Khai Ngup replied, "My friends have gone crazy. I left them in the forest because they kept grinning and wouldn't get up." The king found it strange and sent one of his men along with Ai Khai Ngup to the jungle to find out what happened.

As soon as the man looked at the two bodies he said, "Your friends are dead. Their bodies emit a foul odour."

After the man had left to report the matter to the king, Ai Khai Ngup sniffed himself. *I too smell bad. I must be dead.* He went and lay down on his stomach over a bush as if he were dead. After a little while, a procession of dancers passed that way. One of them stopped by the bush and enquired, "What are you doing lying down in that position?"

"I'm dead," Ai Khai Ngap replied, without moving.

"If that were true, you would not be talking. Come, join us," the man laughed. It did not take too much coaxing to get Ai Khai Ngup up and about. "I'm not dead!" he shouted joyfully, and danced in gay abandon. Ai Khai Ngup went along with the procession of dancers to a house near the river where they all had a sumptuous feast.

After everyone had gone their separate ways, Ai Khai Ngup took a walk along the river bank thinking of his two friends. He felt lost and lonely without them. His thoughts were interrupted by loud slapping sounds coming from ahead. Craning his neck over the bank he saw a girl washing clothes on a large stone slab down below. She was beating the clothes with a stout stick, dipping them into the water and beating them all over again. He stood behind a tree and watched her go about her work. The girl turned back to look him in the eye and shouted, "Instead of standing there watching me, you could help me beat the clothes. I'll give you some food in return."

Having nothing better to do, Ai Khai Ngup went down the bank to the girl and took the stick from her. He beat the clothes for the girl and after she had rinsed and wrung them dry, she gave him some food to eat.

"I must remember that beating gets me food," he mumbled to himself as he walked along. On the way he came across an old couple arguing with one another. They soon came to blows. Ai Khai Ngup sided with the old man and together they beat the old woman till she fell down dead.

Instead of being grateful, the old man blamed Ai Khai Ngup for his wife's death. "You should have separated us instead of joining in the fight. Now look what you did. You killed my old woman," the old man shouted angrily.

"I must remember to separate others when they fight," Ai Khai Ngup repeated to himself over and over again. He walked a little distance when he saw two bulls locking horns and kicking dust.

He yelled at them to stop fighting, but they were far too engrossed in their own battle to listen to him. Ai Khai Ngup walked up to the snorting bulls and tried to separate them. Needless to say, all his efforts were in vain and that was the sad end of poor Ai Khai Ngup.

9

Nang Champu & Chow Manong

Long, long ago, there lived a lonely princess named Nang Champu, whose astrological chart predicted that she would one day be kidnapped. Her parents worried day and night and kept constant vigil over their precious daughter.

Nang Champu had no friends to play with. She grew up chasing the birds and butterflies in the palace gardens under the watchful eyes of a trusted old maid. From the confines of her garden which overlooked the city, the little princess would wistfully watch other children play.

"Why can't I have friends to play with?" she would ask her maid every now and then. The answer would always be the same.

"Because a wicked man will carry you away, and if that were to happen, the king and queen will forever weep." The fear of the wicked man was so great that Nang Champu did not trust any male strangers.

She grew up to be a charming young woman and the king and queen decided it was time for her to get married. They consulted the family astrologer to help them find the perfect match from a host of eligible suitors. The princess however was certain that her future husband would turn out to be the wicked man who would take her away from home, leaving her poor parents in tears. She showed her parents a huge boulder and told them she would marry the person who could cast the stone beyond a certain point. Many hopefuls from far and wide tried their luck but were unsuccessful. It looked like the princess was destined to remain a spinster.

One day, as Nang Champu was strolling in the garden, a Phephai appeared out of nowhere and carried her off into the forest. Her maid had been looking the other way and did not see what had happened. The Phephai kept her imprisoned in a cave and fed her the choicest of fruits and nuts, but the princess was too upset to eat any of it. Everyday the Phephai and his family members came to inspect her. They ogled at her as though she were a tasty morsel.

"She has not gained any weight yet! She requires more food," he would tell his impatient brethren and ply her with more food. The princess knew the Phephai was fattening her up for a family feast where she would end up being the main course. She lived from moment to moment in fear and anxiety.

Not very far away, a prince by the name of Chow Manong was journeying home from his travels abroad. He stopped to rest for the night and in his dreams saw a beautiful princess and a gleaming sword. He woke up with a start and was surprised to find a sword next to him, exactly like the one he had seen in his dream.

"It must be a gift from the Gods," he exclaimed, lifting the gleaming sword.

Mounting his horse, he rode across open country and into the forest until his horse came to a halt. No amount of coaxing would persuade the animal to move forward. Chow Manong quickly dismounted, his senses on full alert. He heard the faint sounds of sobbing coming from within a cave to his left. Peering into the pitch black darkness he could see an iron door with a huge lock.

"Who is it? Are you a human being or a spirit?" Chow Manong called out.

Mistaking the prince for a Phephai, the princess answered, "If you intend to eat me, be done with it. I would rather die than live in constant fear."

"I am not a Phephai. I am a man," Chow Manong replied in a reassuring tone. He was sorry for whoever was inside the cave.

"If you are indeed a man, please open the door and set me free," the princess cried out.

Chow Manong entered the cave and with a sweeping movement of his sword, cut the iron bars as though they were made of grass. He took the princess by the hand and just as they were coming out of the cave, a horde of Phephais arrived. They charged forward, screaming and shouting. Chow Manong swung his sword and cut off the heads of two Phephais in a single stroke. He swung it a second time and killed another four. The remaining Phephais withdrew when they saw they were no match for the prince and begged for their lives, offering their services to him.

"Spare us and we shall do as you say," they begged. Chow Manong being unfamiliar with the terrain asked to be shown the way home. The Phephais cleared the forests and escorted the prince and the princess through a long stretch of hills and valleys till they reached the banks of the river Namlong.

"This is as far as we can go," the Phephais said. They gathered fruits from the nearby forest and offered them to the prince and princess before leaving. The river was too deep and swift for the horse to cross in the dark, so they decided to spend the night in the forest.

It so happened that a hunter chanced upon them while they were asleep. He crept closer to have a look at their faces, clearly recognizable in the bright moonlight. *"She looks like the princess Nang Champu,"* he thought excitedly. *"I must report this to the king."*

The hunter crossed the river from the shallow end and galloped at full speed towards the palace. The king was furious at being woken up in the middle of the night, but his mood changed after hearing what the man had to say.

"Is it true that the person you saw was my daughter?" the king asked.

"Your majesty, it is true. My eyes do not deceive me for I have seen the princess before," the hunter replied. The king summoned his brother and instructed him to bring his daughter back.

The hunter led the uncle and his men into the forest where they found the prince and princess fast asleep. The uncle picked up the sword lying next to the prince, but the touch of the metal felt like burning hot coals, and he threw it away.

"Arrest the man," the uncle commanded the soldiers. The prince woke up to find himself being tied hand and foot like a common criminal. He struggled to free himself but to no avail. "What is the meaning of this?" he asked.

"You are under arrest for kidnapping the princess," the uncle replied.

"No! That is not true," Nang Champu ran forward. "It was he who rescued me from the Phephais. Untie him at once."

"We will decide what is to be done once we get home," the uncle said.

Chow Manong was imprisoned and the princess sent to her quarters and forbidden to meet him. Unable to convince either her father or her uncle, Nang Champu wrote a letter to the prince's father informing him of his son's captivity. She called her trusted maid and told her to deliver the letter to the prince's father.

When Chow Manong's father read the letter, he flew into a rage. "They shall pay with their lives!" he said. "I will myself lead the army against them."

The army commander was summoned and asked to prepare his troops for battle. The king himself led a large army and took the enemy by surprise. A fierce battle was fought and the city was set afire. Taken unawares, Nang Champu's uncle was one of the first to die in battle, leaving his troops in disarray.

Nang Champu wondered whether she had done the right thing by writing that letter and inviting war upon the innocent people of her kingdom. The fire had spread to the palace and in the ensuing commotion, Nang Champu rushed to the prison and set Chow Manong free.

"Your father's men have entered the city," she told him as they hurried along the passages towards the exit. When they came out, loud cheers from Chow Manong's troops greeted them. Nang

Champu's parents had been arrested and Chow Manong's soldiers had taken control over the kingdom.

Chow Manong begged his father to pardon Nang Champu's father. The victorious king at first did not agree, but realizing that it was Nang Champu's letter that had secured the release of his son, he relented. Chow Manong and Nang Champu were married and lived happily.

10

The Three Answers

Seng was the son of a very poor fellow who sold leaf plates for a living. Since there was not much demand for it, they often went hungry. In course of time the old man expired and Seng was left all alone, for he had no relatives in the village. One night Seng saw a very beautiful girl in his dream. Seng could neither forget the girl's face nor the dream. He left his village to seek his fortune in the city, with only a few coins in his possession.

Along the way he witnessed a very peculiar sight. A corpse had been dug out of the grave and was being flogged by an angry looking man. Seng approached the man and asked, "Why are you flogging this dead man?"

"He owes me money and since he is in no position to repay me, I'm punishing him," was the terse reply.

Seng could not bear to stand and watch. "Stop it!" He told the man. "Take all my silver and let the poor soul rest in peace." He dug into his pocket and took out all the coins he had. The man gave him a funny look, took the silver and went off. Seng buried the dead man and continued on his way. He had no money left and wondered where his next meal would come from, but not once did he regret his decision.

As he trudged along, a fellow traveller named Taiko asked Seng if he could join him, since he too had left home to seek his fortune. Together they walked through an endless stretch of paddy fields where storks fed on the little fishes in the canals. Taiko stopped to pluck a few feathers off the birds and put them in his pocket. "They'll come in handy," he explained.

They walked for days, occasionally stopping to rest under the shade of trees, before they finally reached the city where they took up lodgings with an old couple. Seng had no money, but he need not have worried because Taiko insisted on paying for everything. After a wash and a hearty meal, they went to bed and fell asleep almost immediately.

They woke up early to explore the city. There were hardly any people on the streets at that hour and the markets were yet to open. Suddenly there was the clattering of hooves on the street. An extremely beautiful girl dressed in black rode past on a white stallion. For a moment Seng thought he knew her from somewhere. Then he remembered his dream. It was the very same girl from his dreams, only now she was for real.

They asked the sweeper on the street if he knew who the rider was. "That's the emperor's daughter. She goes riding every morning," answered the sweeper.

Why would I dream of her if she has no part to play in my life? Seng wondered, determined to find out more about the princess. When the old woman in whose house they stayed overheard them discussing the princess, she was aghast. "Don't be foolish, young man. You should forget her if you value your life!"

"Why?" asked Seng. "What do you know of her?"

The old woman lowered her voice and said, "She has caused the deaths of half the male population in this kingdom. After all she is the emperor's daughter and she can decide who should live and who should die. People call her the princess of death."

Seng was just about to ask more, when drumbeats on the street outside interrupted them. "That's the king's messenger doing his rounds. Go and listen to what he has to say," the old woman told Seng. The two friends went outside and joined the large crowd that had gathered around the drummer. He stopped beating his drum to make his announcement in a loud voice.

"To all the people of this land, I bring you a message from your emperor. His Majesty is offering the hand of his beautiful

Taiko stopped to pluck a few feathers off the birds and put them in his pocket. "They'll come in handy," he explained.

daughter, the princess Nang Mokya to any man who can read her thoughts. Is there anyone here who is man enough to try his luck?"

"This is my chance to win the hand of the princess!" Seng nudged his friend. Taiko looked on helplessly, knowing it was useless trying to dissuade him.

The old woman was more forthright. "You don't stand a chance," she said. "Do you realize you will lose your head if you are unable to give the correct answer? It's not worth risking your life."

"I have to take a chance. I don't even care if I die trying," Seng answered.

That night, while Seng lay in bed dreaming of the princess, Taiko sneaked out and headed for the palace. He found his way to the bedroom of the princess and waited patiently. At around midnight, Taiko saw a winged chariot glide in through the wide-open windows and land in the bedroom. The princess got up from her bed and went to sit on the chariot, which took off almost immediately. Taiko followed the chariot unseen.

The chariot flew above the clouds and descended into a swirling mist. The princess got off the chariot and walked towards a cave where scorpions, snakes and monsters slithered and crawled around a wrinkled old man seated upon a stool. Nang Mokya smiled and stretched out a dainty hand towards the old man. He got up and they danced, slowly at first and then faster and faster until they became a blur. The monsters joined them in a frenzy. Taiko watched the bizarre scene unfold before him. When the dance was over, the old man went back to his seat while Nang Mokya stood before him.

"I have one more suitor," she told him. "What shall I ask him tomorrow?"

Taiko moved closer and he heard the old man say, "Think of your shoe. He would never dream of that." Nang Mokya nodded and hugged the old man before walking back to the waiting chariot.

It was morning when Taiko returned to find Seng getting

ready to leave for the palace. Taiko pulled Seng aside and almost in a whisper told him, "Your answer to the question will be 'Your shoes'."

"What if that's not the correct answer?" asked Seng.

"It is!" Taiko replied. "Do as I tell you and don't utter a word more."

Seng was ushered into a large hall filled with curious spectators. There was a raised platform with a throne in the center at the other end of the hall. The princess arrived, dressed in all her finery and wearing golden sandals. As soon as she sat down on the throne she called for Seng.

"Tell me what I am thinking of at this moment. If your answer is incorrect you will lose your head," she said imperiously. "If... however, your answer is correct... you may consider yourself lucky to sit beside me."

With as much confidence as he could muster Seng came forward and said, "Your shoes." The princess looked stunned for a moment, then regaining her composure she snapped, "Come back tomorrow for the second round." Getting up from her seat, she stomped angrily out of the hall.

That night Taiko visited the palace again and the same incident occurred. The princess flew off in the winged chariot and met the old man in his cave. They danced together with the monsters and when it was time to leave the princess complained, "My whole body aches as if someone has beaten me. Tell me, what shall I ask tomorrow?"

"Think of your cat," the old man advised. "He was just lucky the first time."

Taiko gave Seng the answer when he met him the next day. Seng did not think of questioning his friend for he somehow knew he could trust him. When Seng entered the hall many strangers in the audience greeted him, saying they wanted him to win. It was a long time before the princess made her appearance. She looked tired and cross. "What am I thinking of now?" She demanded to know as soon as she had taken her seat.

Seng took a deep breath before he spoke. "Your cat!" The princess was livid. How could this simpleton have guessed her thoughts?

"Tomorrow will be the final round and maybe you won't be so lucky this time," she said frostily as she got up to leave. The audience cheered and wished Seng all the luck for the next round.

Seng could not sleep well that night. He tossed and turned and called out to Taiko, but found that his friend was not in his bed. "I wonder where he's gone. I hope he's here on time to tell me the answer tomorrow," Seng worried.

Taiko, at that moment was far away in the land of swirling mists, in search of the third and final answer. The princess complained to the old man of terrible aches and pains. "It feels as if I have been slapped and beaten about," she sobbed. "Tomorrow I will be forced to marry the man if he gives the correct answer. What shall I do?"

"This time think of something no man has ever seen," the old man said. "I shall now accompany you home to make sure that no spy has been following you." Together they flew towards the palace of the princess. After the princess had alighted, the chariot was gliding out the window when a sword appeared out of nowhere and sliced off the old man's head.

Next morning, Taiko handed Seng a bundle and instructed

him on what to do with it. "Do not open it until the princess demands an answer to her question," he cautioned.

This time the hall was packed with eager spectators. Even the emperor and empress were present for the occasion. No one had ever reached the third round before. Seng was dressed in rich silks, which Taiko had provided. They were both sure of a wedding taking place between Seng and the haughty princess once the answer was given.

The princess was confident that this time it would be impossible for the man to answer her question. She threw her head back and taunted Seng, "Well... you've managed to come this far. Others have lost their heads on the first day itself. What do you suppose is on my mind just now?"

All eyes were focused on Seng as he slowly unwrapped the bundle he was carrying. The audience gasped in horror as they watched him lift the severed head of the old man by the hair and hold it aloft for all to see. "Is this what you were thinking of, princess?"

The princess grew pale and fell into a swoon. The emperor and empress rushed to her aid. Her maids fanned her and sprinkled water on her face but the princess lay still as death.

Taiko took out the feathers he had kept in his pocket and waved them over the princess, muttering words that were strange to the ears. The princess slowly woke up as if from a deep sleep.

"Mother! Father! Where am I?" she asked. "What is going on here?" Everyone present was amazed at the turn of events, including Seng.

Taiko came forward and spoke, "The princess was under the spell of the old man who was actually an evil puhsu. She was made to entice young men and get their heads cut off when they failed to answer her impossible questions. The puhsu would then feast on the bodies of the dead men."

"How do you know all these things?" a bewildered Seng asked.

"Do you recall giving all your money to a stranger so that he would stop beating a corpse? Well, I am the dead man you saved from that terrible beating and I took the form of Taiko so that I could repay my debt to you. Being spirit, the princess could not see me as I followed her everywhere. Neither could the puhsu for all his powers! I tried to make the princess come to her senses by beating her every time she boarded the chariot, but the spell was too strong. It could only be broken with the death of the puhsu." Suddenly everything began to make sense to Seng.

"Had it not been for you, none of this would have been possible," Seng told his friend. "I am indebted to you."

The emperor was relieved to have got his daughter back to her former self and wasted no time in marrying her off to Seng and declaring him heir to the throne.

"I'm certain that you will make a good king some day," Taiko told him. "As for me, I have to go."

"Please stay on as my advisor," Seng pleaded. Taiko shook his head. "I have overstayed my visit. I need to go and take a long, long rest." And that is exactly what Taiko did, for no one reported seeing him ever again.

11

The Coconut Fairy

There once lived a very hard working farmer and his wife who had no children of their own. The Gods took pity on them and sent an angel down in the form of a beautiful baby boy. The farmer and his wife were overjoyed and took great pains to see that their son lacked for nothing. They named him Chow Malakungini.

Chow Malakungini grew up listening to stories about fairies, witches and dragons and loved visiting his grandmother for she always had a good story to tell. At a time when boys his age were running around shooting at birds with their slingshots and diving into the river from treetops, Chow Malakungini went about looking for fairies. He peered into birds' nests, flowers, hollow tree trunks and bushes hoping to chance upon an unsuspecting fairy. Even though he was unsuccessful in his attempts, he never gave up hope.

"Are there real fairies?" he asked his grandmother. She gave him a surprised look and said, "They are as real as you and me. The only difference is they don't reveal themselves to everyone."

"Grandmother, have you seen a fairy?" Chow Malakungini asked excitedly.

"If I didn't see them, would I talk about them?" she laughed, patting his head. "Now go! Look carefully and you will find your fairy." Chow Malakungini took his grandmother's advice very seriously and went on looking for his elusive fairy.

When he was old enough, his parents thought it was time for

him to settle down. Being the only son, they went to great lengths looking for a suitable bride for him. All the most beautiful and accomplished girls in and around the village were singled out and shown to Chow Malakungini for his approval, but his answer was always the same.

"I will marry none but a fairy," he sighed.

"How can an ordinary man hope to marry a fairy? Have you gone mad?" his mother wailed. All her pleas fell on deaf ears for Chow Malakungini's mind was made up and he was not about to change it.

His father decided to wash his hands off him saying, "Go and find your fairy bride. If you fail to do so, you might as well drown yourself."

Chow Malakungini left home, promising himself that he would not return until he had found his fairy. He had no idea of where to look so he went wherever his fancy took him. On the way he came across a sage who was deep in meditation. Chow Malakungini sat at the feet of the sage and when the sage finally opened his eyes, he asked him what he wanted.

"I seek a fairy bride," replied Chow Malakungini. "Where will I find her?"

The sage listened patiently and said, "Go towards the east. Turn neither right nor left even if you are tempted."

Chow Malakungini followed the advice of the sage and walked eastward. The road became narrower and branched off towards his right and left into two wide avenues. In front of him lay a steep climb up a rocky path with thorny bushes that closed in on both sides. Chow Malakungini was tempted to take the smooth road leading north but he remembered the words of the sage and resisted the urge. Taking a deep breath he started the climb up the narrow path crying out in pain every time the thorns tore at his flesh. By the time he found himself out of the jungle of thorns his body was covered with scratches and his clothes were in shreds.

Further down the road he met another sage. This one said,

"If you continue going in the same direction, you will find what you are looking for."

"Where will I find her?" Chow Malakungini asked excitedly.

"She lives inside a coconut. You will not miss it if you follow my advice and go east. However, you must wait for the coconut to ripen," the sage replied. "Patience will bring you the happiness you seek."

The sage gave him food and water and a fresh change of clothes. He also gave Chow Malakungini an ointment that soothed the cuts he received from the thorns.

Chow Malakungini was beside himself with excitement. At long last his dreams were about to come true! He could not wait to find his fairy. Thanking the sage for his help and advice he set off on his mission with renewed vigour. Before he even knew it, he came to a clearing where a solitary coconut tree grew. From this tree hung a single coconut that emitted a radiant glow. Around the tree was a group of fierce looking Phephais who appeared to be guarding it. Chow Malakungini hid behind a bush and watched the Phephais as they ate, drank and quarreled amongst themselves. Every now and then they would look up at the luminous coconut as if to assure themselves that it was safe. Just as dawn was about to break, the Phephais became lethargic and one by one they dropped off to sleep. Soon the entire forest reverberated with the sound of their loud snoring.

Finding it safe to venture forth, Chow Malakungini came out from his hiding place and tiptoed towards the coconut tree. He climbed up the tree as quietly as he could and stretched out his hand to pluck the coconut.

"I'm not yet ready to be plucked," a voice from inside the coconut said. Chow Malakungini was now in two minds. Should he or should he not pluck the coconut? Having come this far he did not want to go back empty handed. On an impulse Chow Malakungini plucked the coconut, ignoring the advice of the sage.

Holding his precious coconut, Chow Malakungini moved stealthily away from the coconut tree and the sleeping Phephais.

"My home is not yet mature. If you had waited to open it, I would have had all my jewels and kingdom right here," her melodious voice sounded disappointed.

After he had covered a great distance, Chow Malakungini sat down and carefully split the coconut open. From inside it emerged the most beautiful girl he could ever have imagined. Dressed in shimmering white, her face was as fresh as a newly opened flower. She looked so fragile it seemed the wind might blow her away. At last he had found his coconut fairy.

"My home is not yet mature. If you had waited to open it, I would have had all my jewels and kingdom right here," her melodious voice sounded disappointed.

"I have no need for your kingdom or your jewels," Chow Malakungini assured her. "It is you I have searched for all my life and I want nothing more."

"You seem to be a good man," the coconut fairy said. "You are lucky the Phephais didn't see you."

"Why were they guarding you?" Chow Malakungkini asked her.

"They were waiting for me to mature so that they could marry me off to their king," she answered. "I could hear them discussing all their plans. I'm glad you saved me from those horrible creatures."

Chow Malakungini was eager to take her home and show her off to his parents and everybody else, but it was a long walk to his village. She appeared too delicate to be able to undertake such a long and arduous journey. What could he do?

"I feel a little strange after being woken up before my time," she replied. "I think I need to rest a while."

"Sit here my dear. I shall go home and bring all my family and friends to receive you with the greatest honour as befits a fairy princess," he said, brushing away the leaves from a grassy mound by the river bank.

The coconut fairy sat on the grass and sighed. "I think I shall feel better by the time you return." After seeing that she was comfortable, Chow Malakungini bade her goodbye and went on his way to inform his parents. He kept looking back at his lovely coconut fairy until she was out of view.

Unknown to either of the two, a wicked forest woman had been watching them from behind the trees. The woman found Chow Malakungini so handsome that she wanted to marry him. The only hurdle seemed to be the fairy. As soon as Chow Malakungini was gone, the wicked woman confronted the coconut fairy and forcibly took away her beautiful garments. She pushed the hapless fairy into the river and watched her being swiftly carried away by the currents. Satisfied with her foul deed, the woman sat down on the grassy mound and hummed a happy tune as she waited for Chow Malakungini to return.

When Chow Malakungini reached home his parents were delighted to have him back. "Have you found your fairy princess?" his father asked jokingly.

"Yes, that's why I've come back," he replied and told them all about the coconut fairy. It was an incredible story but it was true.

Preparations were made to receive the bride and a wedding party was sent along with the groom to go and fetch the coconut fairy. Everyone was eager to see the fairy of whom Chow Malakungini spoke in such glowing terms. Surely, this was one wedding no one wanted to miss. His mother took out the jewels and the wedding clothes she had secretly kept aside for her future daughter-in-law. The house was brimming with friends and relatives and the kitchen fires burned throughout the night.

When Chow Malakungini returned to the river bank he was shocked to see an ugly woman instead of the beautiful fairy he had left behind. Where was she? Could she have turned into this ugly woman? The dress was the same and yet...Chow Malakungini's mind was filled with doubts. His companions were surprised when they saw the bride. They began to wonder at Chow Malakungini's definition of beauty.

"Where has she gone?" he asked. "Who are you?" The woman before him burst into tears. "Have you forgotten me already? You took me out of my home and now you ask me who I am." Chow Malakungini was in a dilemma. He was sure this was not the fairy he had left behind. On the other hand, her appearance could have changed because she was plucked before she could mature. He didn't know what to do.

"Come on, why are you making her cry?" His companions intervened. We'd better hurry back before it gets dark." It was with a heavy heart that Chow Malakungini took his bride home. There was no joy left in his heart. When his parents saw their daughter-in-law they were sorely disappointed, but did not voice their feelings. Was it for this harsh looking woman that their son had waited all these years? They noticed that their son was not as happy as he had been when he came home to inform them.

Despite the fact that he felt no love for the woman, Chow Malakungini married her. Those present at the wedding noticed that the groom had a sad and troubled expression on his face while the bride beamed with happiness. There was also another guest at the wedding whom nobody noticed. It was the coconut fairy who had taken the form of a pretty little sparrow and followed the wedding procession. It watched sadly from its perch as the Chow Chere tied the sacred thread around the wrists of Chow Malakungini and the woman, symbolizing their marriage.

The sparrow tried to tell Chow Malakungini that he had been cheated but she could never find him alone for the woman never left his side. One day Chow Malakungini was sitting all by himself and thinking of the beautiful coconut fairy and how she had turned into an ugly woman when the sparrow began to sing. Lost in a world of melancholic thoughts, Chow Malakungini did not pay attention to the bird, but when he heard his name being repeated again and again, he stopped to listen.

Chow Malakungini found himself a fairy bride
And left her by the riverside;
Soon upon the scene there came
A woman so evil, Death be her name;
The fairy to a watery grave that went was I
And Death became his bride, Cry, Malakungini cry!

It slowly dawned on Chow Malakungini that the woman he had married was not his coconut fairy but an imposter. The wicked woman had killed his fairy bride and taken her place. He could not bear it any longer. He called out to his false bride and made her confess to her crime in front of the elders. The wicked woman was put in a basket and thrown into the river. The sparrow was never heard or seen again, and Chow Malakungini still dreamed of his fairy princess, although he knew she would never return.

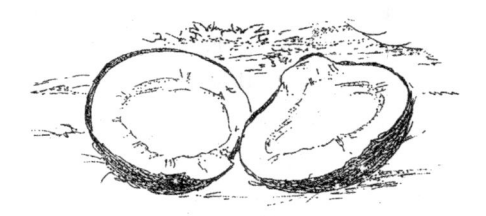

Chow Chere: Pujari, one who conducts religious ceremonies

12

Phanthoi & Tiger

Phanthoi, the biggest conman and Tiger had struck up a friendship of sorts. Tiger was a loner and the other animals in the jungle gave him a wide berth. Phanthoi was a loner too and it seemed the only one in the whole wide world who wasn't scared of Tiger. His wit and intelligence plus the fact that he showed no fear of Tiger earned him Tiger's respect. Sometimes of course Phanthoi acted a bit too smart for Tiger's liking, which made Tiger really mad, but most of the time they got on rather well.

They both were in the habit of carrying walking sticks. Phanthoi had a modest one made of cane while Tiger had a fancy looking golden stick. Phanthoi would have liked to exchange his cane for Tiger's golden stick, but Tiger was very possessive about his walking stick because it commanded awe from the other beasts in the jungle. It made Tiger feel very regal too.

One day, Tiger killed a deer and the two friends made preparations to cook the meat. "Friend Tiger, why don't you go and fetch the water while I light the fire?" Phanthoi said and promptly handed Tiger a pot with a hole in the bottom. Tiger happily strolled down to the stream and began to fill the pot. When he pulled it out of the water, the water level was way down below, so he dipped the pot into the stream again... and again.

"What kind of wretched pot is this? When will it fill up?" Tiger grumbled loudly.

A little bird watching Tiger from the branch above noticed

Phanthoi had been busy digging shallow pits in the ground and burying the meat in them.

the hole in the bottom of the pot and sang...
  Koot-koot! Kooo...oooh..
  Tiger gets a bottomless pot to fill
  While Phanthoi makes off with the kill;
  Koot-koot! Kooo...oooh..

"Will you stop making all that noise?" Tiger roared in anger. The bird did not pay heed to Tiger and continued singing the same song over and over again no matter how much Tiger growled in protest. Unable to stand it any longer, Tiger picked up a stone lying nearby and aimed it at the bird. The stone hit the bird on the foot and injured it, thus putting an end to its singing, much to Tiger's relief.

The foolish tiger went back to filling his pot until his patience wore thin. He finally checked the pot and found that there indeed was a hole in the bottom. The poor bird was telling him the truth then, he realized. No wonder the pot was never getting filled. Tiger got into a really bad mood. He rushed off with a savage roar swearing to find Phanthoi and punish him.

Meanwhile Phanthoi had been busy digging shallow pits in the ground and burying the meat in them. He filled dung in some of the pits and marked them. He had just finished filling up the last pit when Tiger announced his return with an angry snarl.

"What is the idea of giving me a pot with a hole on it? And where is all the meat?" Tiger demanded angrily, looking around and seeing no sign of the deer he had killed.

"How was I to know the pot had a hole in it? And as for the meat, I buried it to keep it fresh," Phanthoi replied.

"Well, I'm hungry now and I want to eat my share. Show me where you've hidden all the meat," Tiger growled impatiently.

Phanthoi took Tiger's golden stick and poked it into the pits where dung was buried, lifted it and shrieked, "Cheeyh! Your stick is useless! It turns meat into smelly dung."

He then took his bumble cane and jabbed it into the pits with meat in them, lifted up chunks of meat and shouted joyfully, "Look! My stick gets me meat. It's a useful stick." He looked at the bewildered Tiger and said, "Don't feel bad, friend Tiger. I'm willing to exchange my good stick with your bad one, after all you need meat more than I do."

Before Tiger realized what he was up to, Phanthoi grabbed the golden stick and ran off. He went and sat next to a giant beehive. Meanwhile Tiger was busy prodding around with Phanthoi's walking stick. He discovered he had been tricked when the stick brought out no meat except smelly dung.

Tiger caught up with Phanthoi in a couple of leaps and bounds. "You've cheated me by taking my golden stick," he said accusingly. "I want it back." Phanthoi pretended not to hear. "Can't you see I'm busy?" he said impatiently.

Tiger was puzzled. Phanthoi did not look busy in the least as far as Tiger could see. He was just sitting there staring at a huge brown lump that was producing a strange humming sound. Tiger had never seen anything of this kind before and it aroused his curiosity. "What's that thing by the way?" he pointed to the beehive.

"That's my grandfather's gong. He told me to guard it." Phanthoi replied.

Tiger came nearer to have a closer look. It was an interesting looking gong by all standards. "Can I beat your grandfather's gong?" he asked.

"Oh! I'll have to ask him," Phanthoi replied, going a little distance and raising his voice. "Grandfather! Friend Tiger wishes to beat your gong." Then, a moment later Phanthoi spoke for his grandfather in a deep baritone, "Tell him that if he must beat it, he should beat it with all his might."

Phanthoi came back and said, "Did you hear what my grandfather had to say? Go ahead and do exactly as he says. Beat the gong with all your might."

Tiger stood on his hind toes, gripped the cane and hit the beehive with all his might. The very next instant he was attacked by an angry swarm of bees that soon had him covered from head to toe. Tiger ran hither thither, roaring in agony and pain with the bees buzzing around him in circles and stinging him mercilessly.

Phanthoi ran nimbly across a rotten old bridge over the raging river and waited nervously on the other bank. Seeing Tiger thrashing about wildly on the grass, he wondered whether he had gone too far this time.

It was quite sometime later that Tiger was able to shake off the vengeful bees. He was still smarting from the painful stings when he spotted Phanthoi resting against a tree on the other bank.

"What do you think you're doing on the other side? I'll come across the river and this time I'll eat you up," Tiger growled.

"This bridge belongs to my grandfather. I'll have to ask his permission before you can walk across," Phanthoi yelled back.

He moved a little distance away and shouted, "Grandfather! Friend Tiger wishes to walk across your bridge." Then he spoke for his grandfather in a deep baritone, "Tell him that if he must walk across my bridge, he should jump and stomp while crossing."

"You have my grandfather's permission. Just remember to

jump up and down as you cross," Phanthoi yelled from the other side.

Tiger braced himself. He jumped and landed on the bridge with a thud. The rotten planks of the old bridge gave way under him and Tiger fell headlong into the river with a loud splash. Phanthoi as usual had disappeared from view and was nowhere to be seen.

Pharthoi: Cheat/rogue

13

Poo's Wisdom

Long, Long ago along the banks of the river Nam Kiu there lived a lonely old man of ninety, who had no one to call his own. His wife and children had died a long time ago and all that Poo had were memories of his loved ones. As time passed, even those treasured memories were beginning to fade. All his friends had passed on into the spirit world and the younger generation had no time for him.

Poo lived in the same old house that he had been born in. A nice cozy little house with carved wooden doors and railings that were chipped and faded with age. He had a small garden with a huge mango tree that was there ever since the time of his grandfather. Its branches spread out from one end of the garden to the other and it bore the sweetest fruit all year round. If there was anything Poo considered most precious to him, it was his mango tree. The garden was overgrown with tall weeds and grass and the fence was broken but nobody dared steal his mangoes and get away without a tongue lashing from Poo.

The mango tree became a landmark in the village and everyone marvelled at its size and the amount of fruit it produced. Nobody in the village could accuse Poo of being a miser. He distributed the ripe mangoes to all the villagers and he always offered the best ones to the monastery. After all, Poo couldn't eat all the mangoes by himself. It only bothered him when people stole from him.

Most of the time when Poo wasn't minding his precious

mango tree, he would be sitting on the frayed mat in his verandah watching people come to the river to fetch water, have their bath, wash clothes or just sit around gossiping. The river bank was the place where everybody in the village met one another while they went about their daily chores. It was the place where the village children spend most of the day, swimming and chasing one another till the sun went down and it was right next to old Poo's house. The river gave Poo as much as it took from him.

Poo enjoyed watching the children swim and play for it reminded him of his childhood days. He particularly enjoyed watching three clean shaven young boys from the monastery on the opposite bank. They reminded him of his own sons who had died a long time ago. Poo remembered how the boys used to love playing in the water at the slightest opportunity. They would swim across the river sitting astride driftwood pretending they were riding elephants. They played with friends who seemed to spend half their waking hours high up on the branches of the mango tree like noisy monkeys. Then one day the floods came and carried his children away. He never saw them again. His wife went into a shell, refusing to believe her children were gone. She hardly ate or spoke to anyone and died soon after. Ever since, every time the river flooded its banks, Poo thought he could hear the laughter of his lost sons above the roar of the waters.

The three boys were always found loitering around old Poo's garden, particularly close to the mango tree. Every time they saw Poo coming they would shout, "The old man has come," and make a quick getaway. He never could catch them red handed for they bolted like lightening. One day as Poo was in the kitchen preparing his meal, he heard the crack of a breaking branch.

"Who is it?" he called out. "Is it you children? Have you come to steal my fruits?"

"No! We're monkeys," a child's voice answered, followed by loud giggles and scurrying feet. Poo got up and went to the window, just in time to see the culprits. It turned out to be the three little temple boys. Curious to know more about them, Poo went to the monastery and had a talk with the monk. "Whose children are they?" he asked.

Pointing out to the three boys who were sweeping the temple floor, the monk replied, "They're orphans from a nearby village and all of them are first cousins too."

"How did they lose their parents?" Poo wanted to know.

"Their parents died during the floods three years ago," the monk explained. "A lot of people died because it happened all so suddenly in the night. They were washed away in their sleep along with their homes. The boys were lucky. They were at their friend's place, which very fortunately was on higher ground. That's how they escaped." Poo's heart went out to them for he understood their pain. The boys looked slyly at Poo as they went about their work. They did not acknowledge him when he smiled at them. That night Poo dreamt of his sons. He saw them playing with the sand on the river bank and when he went closer, their faces were those of the three temple boys.

The village children continued stealing Poo's mangoes and Poo shooed them off each time he saw them. But he was becoming more and more tolerant. "After all, its only mangoes," he muttered to himself and chose to purposely ignore them at times. The three boys however stayed away for a while. They thought that Poo had gone to the monastery to complain about them to the monk. But being children, they soon forgot their initial scare and started frequenting Poo's garden whenever they thought the old man was asleep.

Poo was happy to know that the boys were back in his garden. He smiled to himself when he heard them whisper, "The old man must be asleep. Let's not make too much noise." They did not see him standing behind the cucumber creeper next to the mango tree. He could see them through the screen of leaves. They were sitting on the branches of the mango tree biting off the peel of the half ripe fruit and spitting them on the ground. So engrossed were the children that they did not notice Poo until he stood directly under the tree. When they saw him they almost fell off the tree in shock.

POO'S WISDOM / 81

"Come here children, let's go to the house and I'll give you some ripe mangoes to eat," said old Poo.

The boys looked at one another and thought the old man had gone mad. Instead of scolding them for stealing his mangoes, the old man was inviting them in. This was most unexpected. The three boys needed no further invitation. They jumped down the mango tree like monkeys and waited for Poo to take them inside.

"Go ahead, I'll follow you," old Poo said in a happy tone.

So engrossed were the children that they did not notice Poo until he stood directly under the tree.

They trotted up the wooden steps ahead of Poo and sat down on the bamboo mat in his verandah.

"Let's play a trick on him," one of the boys suggested. "We'll make him look foolish," They put their scheming heads together and cooked up a plan.

Poo took his time climbing up the steps and was pleased to find the three boys sitting cross-legged and eager. Poo took his seat on the mat opposite the boys and said, "Come on, let's talk first. We'll have the mangoes later."

The first boy said, "Let's all tell a story each. Anyone who does not believe the story will be the storyteller's slave." The old man scratched his head and nodded.

The first boy began his story... "When I was in my mother's womb I longed to eat some tamarind. Since my mother was not fond of tamarind, I waited for her to fall asleep before going out in search of a tamarind tree. I finally found one a long distance away and it had ripe, juicy fruits hanging down from its branches. How my mouth watered just looking at them. It was such a tall tree that I couldn't reach the fruit no matter how high I jumped, so I pulled my big toe and catapulted myself up the tree where I sat and ate to my heart's content. There was no way I could get down from the tree so I borrowed a ladder from a neighbouring field. I climbed down the ladder and returned to my mother's womb without her knowing it."

The boys looked at the old man for a reaction, but it wasn't what they had expected. Poo just nodded wisely. "That was a good story," he said.

It was the second boy's turn to tell a story... "When I was a little boy I wanted to eat fish but didn't know how to catch one, so I went to the river and there I saw the biggest fish there ever was. I returned home, took a burning log and lit a fire under the big fish. After the fish was nicely smoked, I sat under the fish and broke pieces of it and ate the whole fish all by myself." He looked at the old man. "Do you believe my story Poo?"

Old Poo said nothing. He looked at the third boy and told

him to start telling his story.

The third boy cleared his throat and began….. "My uncle and aunt lived in a very tall building. One day while I was there on a visit, my aunt was bathing her newborn son. Quite by accident the baby slipped out of her hands and fell through a hole in the floor. My uncle and aunt ran down the stairs and since the house was really very tall they took a long, long time to reach the ground. When they finally reached the ground they saw an old man with a walking stick approaching them. It turned out to be their baby son who had fallen down during his bath. Now, isn't that amazing?"

There was no reaction from the old man. The third boy asked, "Poo, do you believe all our stories?"

"Yes! All three of you are good storytellers," Poo replied. "Now… listen to my story."

"A long time ago when I was a young man, I had three sons who were about the same age as the three of you. They were my pride and joy. I loved them very much. One day the floods came and I lost all three of them. I knew they would someday return home and I was right. My sons are now sitting here with me." the old man said. "If you believe my story, then you are my lost sons. If you don't believe it, then you become my slaves."

The three boys were in a fix. Should they or should they not believe the old man's story. What was better? Being Poo's sons or Poo's slaves?

"Sons would be better than slaves," they whispered to one another. "We'll be able to eat all the mangoes we want."

"We believe you," they echoed. Poo smiled his toothless smile. He went in and brought out a basket of ripe mangoes, which he placed in front of the boys. "Come on my sons, you may have them," he smiled. "I've been saving them for you."

Poo: Grandfather/old man

14

Phanthoi Outwits the Villagers

Phanthoi the conman, was hungry. He went around begging for food but the villagers chased him away, because he had been caught stealing fruits and vegetables from their garden once too often.

"Well, if they behave this way I'll have to steal from them," he grumbled to himself. "I'll steal their cattle and chicken."

Phanthoi waited for an opportunity to put his plans into action. One dark night he stole two cows and sold them off in another village. Thereafter, he stole hens and ducks to feed himself. He would take them to his hideout and eat them smoked, boiled or dried as was convenient to him. One day as he was about to eat a freshly smoked chicken, he heard Tiger calling out to him. Quick as a flash he put the meat under his bottom and sat down pretending to stoke the fire as Tiger stalked in.

"I can smell smoked meat," Tiger purred, sniffing around the place. "Aren't you going to offer me some of it?"

"The only meat I have is my own," Phanthoi said. "See, I'm going to eat a slice of my own bottom." He lifted one side of his bottom and with his knife sliced off a bit of the chicken underneath and popped it into his mouth. "Mmmm...It's not bad at all," he smacked his lips.

Tiger stared open mouthed. "Now why didn't I ever think of it?" he asked. Phanthoi handed him the knife. Tiger took it and tried to slice off his own bottom but it proved to be too painful. Moaning in agony, Tiger realized he had been made a fool of, when he saw Phanthoi making a quick getaway with a chicken in his hand. To add insult to injury, Phanthoi was laughing so hard he almost tripped.

Tiger was in a vengeful mood. He gave chase. Phanthoi ran towards the village shouting, "Tiger! Tiger! Help! Help!" The villagers rushed out armed to the teeth with spears, swords, stones and sticks. They pelted Tiger with stones and chased it with lighted bamboo torches. After they had succeeded in chasing Tiger away, the villagers returned and found Phanthoi resting under a tree. Unfortunately, one of the villagers recognized him.

"That's the thief who stole my chickens," the man shouted, pointing out to Phanthoi. "Catch him!"

Phanthoi saw the crowd rushing towards him. He got up in a trice and ran as fast as he could with the villagers hot on his tail. He headed for the best hiding place he could think of at that moment. It was an old abandoned porcupine's burrow, just wide enough for him to crawl into. By the time the villagers reached the burrow, Phanthoi was safely inside.

The villagers stood around the entrance to the burrow. One of them bent down to peer in, but it was too dark to see anything. "Let's see how deep the burrow is," another said. He had a coil of bamboo strip, which he proceeded to unwind and push into the burrow. Phanthoi could hear them very well from within. He waited for the bamboo strip to reach him and began to slowly wind it till he felt the end of the strip.

"The hole is too deep. Poor Phanthoi must be dead by now. He surely could not have survived the fall." He heard the villagers discussing, much to his relief.

15

Sangken

Once upon a time when the earth was in its infant stage, its beauty so dazzled the Khunphes and Nangphes of Maungsang that they flew down in hordes to feast upon the delectable fruits of the soft earth.

Lost in its heady fragrance, they grew heavy and lost their ability to fly. By and by memories of their celestial home grew dimmer and dimmer until all was forgotten. Thus were the once mighty gods of Maungsang transformed into earthlings. All except Chow Khunsang, who was able to forgo the pleasures of the earth and make the journey to Maung Phe or Paradise, the abode of the great spirits.

Chow Khunsang quickly mastered the language and customs of Maung Phe and became a respected member of society. Jealous of his popularity, Chow Sekay, the God king of Maung Phe married him off to the sister of Chow Khunkiew, the God of misfortune, misery and disease, hoping that some ill fortune would rub off on him. Chow Khunsang gave his brother-in-law a wide berth for they shared nothing in common. In due course, Chow Khunsang's wife bore him four daughters, the celestial maidens named Kholaka, Maholaka, Nandalak and Tat-Thilaka.

One day, an animated discussion was taking place at the king's court regarding the functioning of the universe. The majority of the gods agreed with the God king's version that the sun revolved around a stationary earth. Those who thought otherwise preferred not to voice their opinion for fear of the God king's wrath. Chow Khunsang however, could not help putting forth his point of view, which was contrary to what was blindly accepted as the truth. His theory was so convincing that it set the council thinking. The God king took it as a personal affront, but he made a show of being a magnanimous and just ruler.

"Why not stand witness to the movement of the stars ourselves instead of arguing?" Chow Sekay proposed to the assembly. It was decided that all the gods would meet at the great platform from where the entire universe would be visible in all its infinite glory.

Chow Sekay sought to teach Chow Khunsang a lesson. Commanding the earth be motionless, he summoned the stars and ordered them to move around the earth at his behest. The stars could not refuse their God king, even if they thought his command inappropriate.

At the appointed hour, all the gods gathered at the platform so as to witness the functioning of the universe. Upon the God king's signal, the sun and stars moved in circles around the still earth, proving Chow Khunsang's theory wrong. Praise was heaped upon the king by his awe-struck audience, who knew not that they had been fooled.

Chow Khunsang realized it was a plot to humiliate him, for he alone knew the truth, but being an outsider and with the entire council opposing him, he had no option but to remain silent. Although Chow Sekay had won the initial round, he still harboured a grudge against Chow Khunsang. He took Chow Khunkiew into confidence and the two devised a plan to get rid of their common enemy. Knowing how impossible it was to heap any misfortune upon his brother-in-law, Chow Khunkiew asked his nieces to find out the secret behind their father's invincibility.

"My hair is my strength as well as my only weakness," Chow Khunsang had once confided in his family. "One single strand if tied to the Khanchak will be sufficient to kill me." His daughters were aware of this family secret for a long time and saw no harm in sharing it with their maternal uncle. So unsuspecting were they of their uncle's treachery that they even handed him a strand of their father's hair when asked for it. Chow Khunkiew now had the ultimate weapon with which to destroy his enemy and promptly passed it on to the God king to use at an opprotune moment.

One day, Chow Sekay and Chow Khunsang got into a heated argument while discussing the astrological method for predicting rain. Neither of them was willing to concede to the other, so they both came down to earth and asked the wise Chow Pingya for his opinion. It was agreed upon that the one whose prediction proved wrong would lose his head.

When the two Gods descended on earth, Chow Pingya was busy ploughing his field. Introducing themselves, they explained the purpose of their visit and requested him to be the judge. Chow

The king of Maungsang ordered the four errant daughters of Chow Khunsang to take the responsibility of holding their father's head in their hands, so as to save the world from destruction and also to atone for their sin.

Pingya through his own calculations came to the conclusion that Chow Sekay was right. Chow Khunsang graciously acceded defeat and accordingly had to forfeit his head. Armed with the secret knowledge that the daughters of Chow Khunsang had given him, Chow Sekay beheaded his rival with the celestial axe 'Khanchak' tied with a strand of his own hair.

When the severed head rolled to the ground, it radiated extreme heat and energy, causing a fire so great that it consumed everything in its vicinity. The fire raged uncontrolled till the Gods of Maungsang had to be called upon to put out the blaze. The Gods kept the severed head suspended in the air, but the intense heat from it evaporated all the clouds and there was drought. They then immersed it in the ocean thinking the waters would cool it, but the heat evaporated the entire ocean and the land was parched and the fishes and all the sea creatures were burnt to a crisp. Nothing the Gods did could contain the destructive nature of Chow Khunsang's head. The only ones who could withstand the intensity of heat emitted from the head were his daughters, for they were of his blood.

The king of Maungsang ordered the four errant daughters of Chow Khunsang to take the responsibility of holding their father's head in their hands, so as to save the world from destruction and also to atone for their sin. Meanwhile they attached the head of an elephant named Elawon on the body of Chow Khunsang in order to give him a new lease of life.

So intense was the heat which radiated from the severed head that none of his daughters could hold it for more than a day. When each day ended, the head was passed on to the next daughter. Since one heavenly day is equal to one earth year, the moment Chow Khunsang's head is passed from one daughter to another, a new earth year is born.

Chow Khunkiew could not reconcile himself to the fact that the gods of Maungsang had resurrected his old enemy and therefore vowed to kill the elephant headed God. It is to achieve this end that he continually spreads misfortune and disease through all the realms. To shield themselves from harm, Khamtis seek the protection of the Lord every new year by observing certain rituals. On this day, the statues of the Buddha are taken out of the temples and placed in a specially constructed shrine where they are showered with scented water from a water fountain. Water is also poured over the Bodhi tree, the ropes of holy manuscripts, the hands of monks, the hands and feet of elderly people and over one another. This festival is called 'Sangken' and is celebrated on the New Year day to invoke the blessings of the Buddha for peace, harmony, good luck, good health and protection from the evil influences of Chow Khunkiew.

Khanchak: Celestial; Khunphe: God; Nangphe: Goddess; Maungsang: The seventh heaven or the highest realm

16

Devotion

There was a very wealthy young man whose treasury was filled to overflowing with gold and silver. He religiously donated up to forty thousand kilos of silver coins every day to the temple. The silver was weighed each day before being carted to the temple. He could have squandered all his wealth, but he chose to give it back to God as a way of showing his gratitude. His devotion to God could not be questioned. Everyone in town held him as an example of goodness.

On the other hand, in the same town there lived an extremely poor man named Chow Tukta who had to care for his aged mother. He was so miserably poor that he had to beg on the streets for a handful of rice just to survive. At the end of each day he would go home and give his mother all the rice that he managed to get and she would cook it for the two of them. His love for his mother was so great that whenever there wasn't enough food for both, he would pretend that he had already eaten so that his mother could eat her fill.

Of course no one knew or bothered to speak highly of Chow Tukta's devotion to his mother. To the world, he was just an ordinary beggar, an irritant to society, to be pelted with stones by children and shouted at by people who had no time for beggars. To the Gods however, his devotion to his mother was comparable to the rich man's devotion to God.

The Gods debated as to which form of devotion deserved greater merit. Was it the rich man who donated this vast sum of money to the temple, or the poor man who sacrificed his food for his mother? It was such a complex issue that the Gods themselves were divided in their opinion.

The two men belonged to the same town, which was part of a vast empire ruled by a virtuous king who had seven daughters, each one prettier than the other. His youngest daughter, Nang Mono was the prettiest and most talented of all the sisters. The Gods who favoured the rich man felt that the rich man deserved to have the accomplished Nang Mono as his wife. On the other hand, the Gods who favoured Chow Tukta thought that it was he who deserved to marry the princess.

Both parties arrived before the king at the same time, with the same intention. They had come to ask for the hand of the princess on behalf of their candidates. The king welcomed them with great humility and asked them to enlighten him on the two young men on whose account they had come.

The Gods in favour of the rich man spoke highly of his generosity and devotion to God. "He is a man of high morals and integrity and therefore will make an excellent match for the princess," they said.

The Gods who had come on behalf of Chow Tukta praised him for his devotion to his mother. "A hungry man who is capable of sacrificing his food for his mother's sake is capable of doing good to all, they said. "The princess could not ask for a more loyal and loving husband."

The king, after hearing both parties, could not decide who was more deserving of the two. He approached the Overlord of Paradise for advice but even he was undecided. Finally, Chow Khunsang the all-knowing stepped forward.

"I can solve the problem, but only on one condition," he said. "What I say will have to be accepted by everyone present."

When all those assembled nodded their heads in agreement, he continued, "I had three mothers and I served them all equally with the greatest devotion. They in turn gave me their blessings and it is because of their blessings, that I was awarded the highest seat in Maungsang. Therefore, serving one's mother selflessly deserves greater merit."

The Gods could not argue with Chow Khunsang's philosophy for they knew he was always right. Ultimately they all came down to earth to seek the hand of Nang Mono on behalf of Chow Tukta. The king very gladly consented to the proposal and the two were married amid great pomp and splendour. The Gods showered the newly weds with all the worldly goods and blessings ensuring them a very happy and comfortable life.

17

The Dragon Princess

A sage sat in deep meditation under a sprawling banyan tree oblivious to the world around him. Nearby, a fierce battle raged between the man-bird Kingnara and a dragon. Seeing there was no escape from his enemy's sharp talons, the dragon fled towards the tree, but Kingnara flew down and plucked him off the ground. The dragon was at the mercy of Kingnara, whose talons gripped and lifted it in the air. The dragon struggled in midair, hissing and spitting fire, causing one of Kingnara's feet to get entangled in the branches of the tree. Kingnara screeched and tried to break free, while holding on to the writhing dragon.

Chow Muksa, a fearless hunter was passing by and witnessed the savage fight. Taking pity on the dragon, he took out his arrow and shot Kingnara, felling him. The dragon was grateful to Chow Muksa for having saved him from the jaws of death.

"Come with me to my kingdom," the dragon told Chow Muksa and escorted him to a city where the streets were paved with gold. The majestic buildings were also all made of gold and intricately carved with images of dragons studded with diamonds and precious gems. Amazingly, the moment the dragon king entered his kingdom, he transformed into a man. There were dragons as well as people in the dragon kingdom. They could transform themselves at will.

Inside the royal palace beautiful maidens came to greet them with flowers, fruits and drink. "Meet my daughter Nang Naka," the king said, introducing the lovely princess standing beside him.

The dragon was at the mercy of Kingnara, whose talons gripped and lifted it in the air.

"Accept her as your wife, along with half my kingdom."

Chow Muksa fell in love with the princess at first sight. She was beautiful beyond comparison and when she smiled, she outshone the brightest jewels in the kingdom. The marriage took place with the entire population of the dragon kingdom present. The princess went to the crystal fountain to offer prayers and seek blessings. The spirit of the fountain, pleased with her devotion, granted her wish to remain in human form for the rest of her life.

Before Kingnara breathed his last, he vowed to seek vengeance on the person who shot him. He asked the sage for a boon. "May I be reborn a man in my next life," he prayed. "To be invincible, to avenge my death."

Taking pity on the dying Kingnara, the sage granted him his wish. He was reborn a man with super human powers and was known as Chow Kingnara. There was no one who could defeat him in battle

As fate would have it, Chow Kingnara entered the dragon kingdom and like all newcomers was impressed with the riches and grandeur of the city of gold. He roamed around the city enjoying the sights and the marvellous buildings. As he looked up to admire the palace, he saw the beauteous Nang Naka standing on her balcony and immediately lost his heart to her. Chow Kingnara could think of nothing else but the face of the beautiful woman he had seen.

"That is the princess Nang Naka, the wife of Chow Muksa," someone informed him. Chow Kingnara was disappointed to hear that the princess was already married and yet he could not forget her. He passed by the palace day after day hoping to see her again. One of the maids noticed him looking up at the balcony every time he passed by and reported the matter to the princess. One day Nang Naka saw him and asked him to leave.

Instead of feeling insulted, Chow Kingnara smiled and said he would come again. That evening Nang Naka related the incident to her husband. Chow Muksa picked up his sword and challenged Chow Kingnara to a duel, which the latter readily accepted. Although Chow Muksa was an exceptional fighter, he was no match against his adversary, who was blessed by the gods themselves.

A large crowd had gathered by the time the princess Nang Naka reached the scene but it was too late, for her husband was already dead. She was so distraught that she did not even weep. Chow Kingnara asked forgiveness from Nang Naka through messengers but she refused to meet them. For a long time the princess kept herself within the confines of her palace to mourn the death of her husband. The lovelorn Chow Kingnara approached the king and asked for Nang Naka's hand in marriage. The king conveyed the message to his daughter, saying he left the decision to her. The princess, after much thought, agreed to the proposal on one condition.

"I will marry him tomorrow itself if he will meet me near the waterfall and do as I tell him to," she said. "That is my only condition."

Early next morning Nang Naka was dressed in her wedding finery. Her maids carried her up the steep mountain on a golden palanquin. Chow Kingnara was already waiting for her to arrive. As soon as Nang Naka got off her palanquin, she held out a golden cup. "Fetch me water in your mouth from the edge of the waterfall and fill this cup," she said.

Eager to prove himself, Chow Kingnara walked to the edge of the waterfall and bent down to fill his mouth with water. From where he stood he could see the entire valley spread out below him.

The beautiful princess raised her arms heavenward and let out a piercing cry. A bolt of blue light shot out of the skies and engulfed her, transforming her into a flaming dragon of many hues. Chow Kingnara raised his head just in time to see the dragon lash out its tail at him. As he fell to his death down the great waterfall, he thought he could see the face of Nang Naka looking coldly down at him from the top of the mountain.

18

Bramawati & Nang Kungtra

Long, long ago when the Nanchows waged wars against their enemies, the great king Bramawati ruled over an extensive kingdom. He was loved and respected by his subjects on account of his fairness and compassion. His wife, the beautiful Nang Kungtra and their two teenage sons were his greatest source of joy.

King Bramawati took regular rounds of his kingdom on the royal chariot in order to see first hand how his people lived. One day it so happened that while the king was on one of his rounds, the chariot brushed against Nang Chanta, who was out hunting for a husband. She was so pre-occupied flaunting her charms to a rich nobleman that she did not see or hear the royal chariot coming, until one of its wheels caught and ripped off her stole.

"Don't you have eyes, young lady?" the king reprimanded her. "Be more careful in future."

Before Nang Chanta realised what was happening, the chariot took off in a cloud of dust. She would never forget this insult for the rest of her life, especially when it took place in front of the man she was out to impress. She was an ambitious girl who relied on her charms to find herself a rich husband. This unfortunate incident made her all the more determined to better her station in life and she eventually married the ageing king of the Kling dynasty.

Due to his advanced age and failing health, the king of Kling and Nang Chanta had no children of their own. They adopted a little girl who had been found lying in the center of a lotus flower and named her Nang Mohom Putungma. Nang Chanta lavished all her love and affection on her, dressing her up in clothes and jewels that she had only dreamed of all her life.

It had long been a tradition with king Bramawati to observe a ceremony lasting three days, in which he gave alms to anyone who approached him. It was now time for that ceremony to take place, so the king sent his messengers to make announcements all over the kingdom. People thronged the palace grounds throughout the day. The generous king did not refuse alms to anyone, even those that came from other kingdoms.

They adopted a little girl who had been found lying in the center of a lotus flower and named her Nang Mohom Putungma.

When Nang Chanta heard of the announcement, an evil plan took shape in her mind. It was now time for her to extract revenge for the insult, which king Bramawati had long forgotten, but she had not. Putting on a woeful expression she related the story to her husband, urging him to help her seek revenge on the king.

Kling was an arrogant person with a large ego and because of the great difference in their age, a very indulgent husband. It did not take much cajoling from his young wife to spur him on. So, he dutifully went to the court of king Bramawati in accordance with his wife's wishes. Bramawati welcomed his guest and enquired if there was anything he could offer him.

"I am old and need someone to look after me. You as a king have promised to give up everything. If you are a true king, you must give me what I have come to ask for," Kling said.

"Do not hesitate," king Bramawati urged kindly. "Ask me for anything and it shall be yours."

"If that be true, then I want you to come with me as my personal attendent," Kling said. There were loud protests and angry outbursts from the king's subjects at this insolent request. The royal guards drew their swords and charged forward, but king Bramawati stopped and silenced them all.

'I have given my word and I shall keep it," he said. "If it is my destiny to be a slave, then so be it." He removed his royal robes and bade farewell to his tearful wife and children before leaving. As soon as they reached the kingdom of Kling, king Bramawati was thrown into a prison cell.

Back in his own kingdom, his queen Nang Kungtra and the two princes were so disturbed by what had taken place that they were at a total loss. The king's Prime minister had long wanted to dethrone the king and this seemed the perfect opportunity to put his plans to action. He proposed marriage to the queen and threatened to poison her two sons if she refused. The elder son Chow Weseng, took his father's sword and challenged the Prime Minister to a duel, but was overpowered by the soldiers loyal to the Prime Minister and taken prisoner. The Prime Minister then stormed into the queen's quarters and ordered her to be prepared to marry him the following day. Chow Kungche, the younger prince swore that he would not rest until he found his brother. He would have gone in search of his brother had his mother not restrained him.

With the help of her faithful maid, the queen and her son escaped from the palace and took cover in the forests. They walked a long way through thick forests before they came to a river bank, where they stopped to rest.

A Phephai in the guise of a woman was rowing a small boat across the river. She stopped by and asked sweetly, "Would you like to go across to the other side?"

Nang Kungtra and the prince knew it would be safer for them to go as far away as possible from their home so they accepted the offer.

"My boat is meant for two people, so I can only take one of you at a time," the Phephai said.

"In that case, my son will go first and you can come for me later," Nang Kungtra replied.

Chow Kungche got into the boat and the Phephai rowed him across to the other bank before making a trip back to pick up his mother. Mid-stream she took the form of Nang Kungtra and turned the boat around. When Chow Kungche saw his mother rowing the boat he was surprised, for he had never seen her do so before.

"Where is the woman who was rowing the boat?" he asked. "How is it that you are rowing the boat all by yourself?"

The Phephai wondered if the prince suspected anything amiss."The woman had some urgent work, so she gave me the oars," she replied in the queen's voice. She got off the boat and suggested they walk towards the forest. When they had gone deep into the forest, the wily Phephai looked coyly at the prince and sang, "There is no one here besides the two of us, so why not son be husband and mother be wife."

Hearing this, the prince grew suspicious. *She definitely is not my mother. It must be a Phephai in the guise of my mother.*

"Don't you like my song?" the Phephai asked the prince when she got no response from him.

"I'm tired and sleepy," Chow Kungche yawned and lay down under a tree. He then pretended to be fast asleep. The Phephai lay next to him and soon her loud snoring took over. Quietly as he could, Chow Kungche got up and made off for the boat. The Phephai's sixth sense woke her up and she gave chase. Chow Kungche was already on the boat and halfway across the river when the Phephai reached the river bank. Unable to cross the river without a boat, she thumped her chest in frustration until she fell down dead.

Chow Kungche could find no trace of his mother on the other bank. He looked all over the place in vain. Then he heard some girlish laughter and went forward to investigate. He saw a beautiful princess along with her attendants having a bath in the river. He also saw one of them picking up a piece of jewelry and hiding it in the folds of her dress.

When the bath was over they all went about changing into their clothes. There was a loud shriek from the princess. "My necklace is missing! Who could have taken it?" The maids went searching all over and discovered Chow Kungche hiding behind a tree.

"He must be the thief," the maid who took the necklace shouted accusingly. They surrounded and searched him but found nothing so they took him alongwith them to the palace. Chow Kungche had no choice. He had no place to go to in any case. When they reached the palace the princess told her father what had happened. The king ordered that Chow Kungche be sent to the stables to look after the horses. The man in charge of the stables was a hard taskmaster who made sure that Chow Kungche worked without a break.

One day, as the princess was leaning out of her window, she saw Chow Kungche carrying a heavy sack to the stables. She noticed that he looked thin and sad. *What was he saying?* The princess strained her ears and overheard him as he lamented his plight. "Even though I am a prince I'm treated like a lowly servant who has to suffer because they prefer to believe thieving maids."

The princess sent for the chief maid and said, "I know it was you who stole my necklace while putting the blame on Chow Kungche." The maid said nothing but her expression betrayed her guilt.

"If you do not confess your guilt, I shall have to send you to the torture chamber," the princess threatened. "Maybe that will make you talk."

"Forgive me your majesty. It was a mistake. I won't repeat it again," the maid begged, falling down on her knees. She promptly returned the missing necklace.

The princess sent for Chow Kungche and apologized to him. "Tell me the truth," she said. "Are you really a prince?"

"I am the son of king Bramawati," he replied and went on to tell her all about his family and himself. She felt extremely ashamed of herself for having falsely accused him of theft and making him work in the stables.

The princess presented him clothes fit for a prince and took him to the king. When the king learnt that Chow Kungche was a prince he tried to make amends by offering him the hand of his daughter in marriage. Chow Kungche had secretly admired the princess and was only too happy to oblige. A grand wedding took place and the king proclaimed him heir to the throne after him.

Meanwhile, Chow Weseng had been languishing behind bars for over fifteen years. He went into deep meditation thus pleasing the Gods who gifted him a magic sword as boon. Wielding the sword, he killed his captors and went out in search of his parents and brother. On the way he encountered an old hag who told him the exact location where his father was held captive. Chow Weseng stormed his way into the palace grounds, killing the guards who tried to stop him, leaving behind him a trail of death and destruction. With his magic sword he cut through the thick iron bars of the prison and found his father frail and white haired, but otherwise in good health.

When the news reached Kling and his queen Nang Chanta that Chow Weseng had forcibly entered the palace, they feared for their lives. They begged him for forgiveness and offered their daughter Nang Mohom Putungma's hand in marriage. Chow Weseng was hesitant but his father urged him to let bygones be bygones and insisted on the marriage. When Chow Weseng met the princess in person, he was captured by her beauty and willingly married her. To make amends for their past mistakes, his in-laws gave him the reins of the kingdom. Kling and his wife retired to the forest to spend the rest of their lives in meditation.

Now that he had found his father, Chow Weseng's next aim was to find his mother and brother. A festival was arranged and messengers were sent to all parts of the kingdom and also to neighbouring kingdoms, to invite each and every individual. The best artists were engaged to paint large portraits of king Bramawati, his wife Nang Kungtra and their sons. These were put up all over the kingdom and rewards announced for any person who could bring news of the queen and Chow Kungche to the king.

Nang Kungtra attended the festival with the hope of meeting her lost son. She found him standing in front of the portrait of King Bramawati and Chow Weseng. Nang Kungtra hugged her son and told him how she had travelled all over looking for him after they had lost each other near the riverbank. Together they went to meet King Bramawati and Chow Weseng and there was great rejoicing at the family reunion.

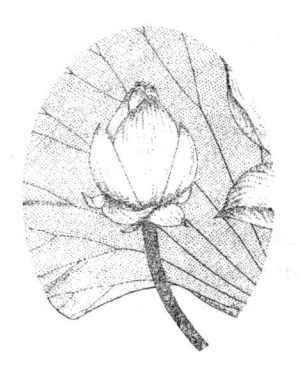

19

The First Yasi

A very poor couple had a daughter who was neither good looking nor talented and therefore destined to live a very hard life. Extremely dissatisfied with her dreary existence, she dreamed all day long of the good things in life. Whenever she saw girls her age in fine clothes, she would burn with jealousy and wish herself in their place.

"Why don't you send me to live with aunt Lin?" she begged of her parents. "They don't have any children and are rather fond of me." Perhaps they would adopt her too, she silently hoped.

All her whining and pleading finally paid off and her parents agreed to let her go. "Be a good girl and help your uncle and aunt. Don't trouble them." Her mother advised.

Her aunt and uncle were more than pleased to have her stay with them in their huge mansion and the young girl took to her new surroundings like a duck takes to water. She was given fine clothes to wear and ate out of fine china instead of leaves, as she used to at her own home. She hoped and prayed that her luck would hold.

One day the God of good fortune came down to earth in the guise of a mendicant, his body barely covered in leaves. The girl, all dressed up in her new clothes, noticed the mendicant shivering in the cold. Without the slightest hesitation, she removed her shawl and offered it to the mendicant. He accepted the offering and said, "For this act of kindness, I grant you a boon. Ask for anything your heart desires."

The girl did not even think twice before she said, "I wish I was rich and beautiful."

"Consider your wish fulfilled," the mendicant raised his hand in blessing and disappeared. The girl waited and waited, but there was no change in her appearance or fortune. Her rich uncle suffered huge losses in business and had to sell his mansion and move into a modest home. They could no longer afford to keep her with them.

The girl returned home to her parents and to her former life of drudgery. She married a poor farmer and spent the rest of her life working in the fields and taking care of her family. In her heart she still carried some hope of riches and glamour till the day she died.

Soon after her death, she reincarnated into the family of a very wealthy merchant. Everyone called her Saophe or heavenly maiden rather than by her own name because she was exceedingly beautiful. As she grew older, she received many offers of marriage but none of them were of any interest to her. On hearing about her exceptional beauty, the king from a neighbouring country despatched three of his courtiers to Saophe's house with a marriage proposal.

A lavish banquet was laid out and served by Saophe. The courtiers were so awe-struck by her beauty that they scarcely knew what they were doing. Their trembling hands knocked the food and drinks about in a clumsy manner and when they tried to eat they messed up their cheeks, noses and chins. They were a disgraceful sight to watch. Embarrassed by the fact that they had made complete fools of themselves in front of Saophe and her family, they decided to mislead the king. They told him that Saophe was of average looks and that the girls in their own kingdom were far prettier. The king was disappointed and thereby lost interest in pursuing the matter further. He married the daughter of a nobleman instead.

Saophe had meanwhile fallen deeply in love with the handsome king whose face she saw in a painting. She wondered what the courtiers had told the king about her. After months of endless waiting, her parents discovered that the king had married someone else. A broken hearted Saophe could not fathom why the king would do such a thing. Why did he reject her when he had not even cast his eyes on her? Did his courtiers find her unsuitable to be a queen? Humiliated and hurt, she blindly married the first man who proposed to her. Her husband Chow Mao was a minister at the king's court. Besides being loving and attentive to his beautiful wife, he was a kind and generous man. Saophe settled down to a comforatable married life.

One day, as Saophe stood on her balcony overlooking the street, she saw the king's procession approaching. As the royal chariot was slowly passing by, the garland of flowers which she was holding slipped from her hands and fell directly on the king. Saophe waited with bated breath to see the king's reaction.

Startled, the king glanced up to see who had thrown it. Their eyes met and he was smitten. He had never before seen anyone as lovely as her. "Who is that angelic beauty? Why did no one tell me about her? She is fit to be a queen," he exclaimed.

"Her name is Saophe," his companion whispered. "She would have been our queen if your majesty had not rejected her. She is now the wife of Chow Mao, the minister."

From that day onwards the king became a slave to his emotions. The lovelorn king could think of nothing else but the beautiful woman on the balcony. He banished the courtiers who had misled him, for had it not been for them, Saophe would have been his queen. He wooed her with precious gifts and ardent letters, unmindful of the fact that his actions drew criticism from friends and foe alike. Saophe received the gifts and letters with dignity and grace, but refrained from replying to any of them. She was flattered and encouraged to spend longer hours in front of the mirror, admiring her beauty and smiling mysteriously. The long suffering Chow Mao could bear it no longer. He asked his wife to choose between the king and him.

Saophe made no comment, not knowing how her life had become so complicated. She wondered if her beauty was a curse rather than a boon, for it had caused the king to forget his duties and behave in a manner so unbecoming. It had heaped shame and sorrow upon her husband. The more she thought about it the more convinced she was that her beauty had become a burden to her. Desperate to find peace, Saophe shaved off her hair and changed into simple clothes. Taking leave of her husband, she retired to the forest where she lived an austere life of meditation and prayer. It is said that Saophe was the first yasi or Buddhist nun.

20

The Turtle Prince

Nang Srichaka was an extremely beautiful princess who thought no end of herself. Her parents had spoiled her to such an extent that she grew up to be the kind of person who had nothing positive to say about others.

When she came of age, there was no dearth of eligible suitors who came to seek her hand. Nang Srichaka poked fun at them and sent them on their way. They were either too short or too tall, too fat or too thin or ugly and so on and so forth. No one seemed worthy of her, it seemed. Her father decided to take matters into his own hands, so he sent a proposal to an old friend who had a son. The friend, who was a king in a far off land, promptly dispatched his son to meet the princess.

The princess's first impression of him was unflattering. "He is so slow he should have been born a turtle."

A spirit who happened to be passing by, overheard the remark and promptly turned the prince into a turtle. The princess gaped open mouthed in surprise and so did the king and all the people assembled there. The turtle crawled clumsily towards the princess, who shrank back in horror.

"Take this creature away from me!" she shrieked. The king stepped forward, purple with rage. "This is your fault daughter," he said accusingly. "You have turned a good man into a turtle. What will I tell my friend?"

"It was a mistake, father," she cried. "I said it in fun."

"You have always had fun at other people's expense," the king shouted angrily. "You will now have to marry this turtle who will henceforth be addressed as Chownoi Tao."

The princess begged and cried till she fell down exhausted, but the king did not relent. The queen was a mute spectator. In any case she never did have much say in any matter whatsoever.

Preparations for the wedding began in earnest. A little hut was erected next to the lotus pond outside the palace grounds. The place was given the name Nong Tao, and the newly wedded couple were to live there, with the princess in the hut and the turtle in the pond. The king wanted the world to know who his son-in-law was, so he sent out invitations to all the kings in the neighbourhood. No one wanted to miss out on this strange union between a princess and a turtle and so the wedding was well attended. After all the guests were fed and seen off with gifts, friends and relatives took the newly married couple to Nong Tao.

As soon as they were left alone, Srichaka took a stick and pushed Chownoi Tao out of the hut and into the pond. He fell in with a loud t'plung!

"That's your home and this is mine," she said rudely, slamming the door shut.

That night the princess did not sleep a wink at all. She sobbed and sobbed in self-pity till her eyes were red and swollen. Chownoi

Tao heard her crying and came out quietly from the water. He went to the door of the hut and stayed there till the sounds of the birds chirping announced the arrival of dawn.

Chownoi Tao was hungry because no one had remembered to give him any food during or after the wedding. He could not help thinking about his favourite foods and to his amazement he saw a big bowl of Pasa and steaming hot rice in front of him. He ate the food with relish and wished he could have saved some for his bride. The moment he thought of it, another bowl of Pasa and rice appeared magically before him. He carried the bowl towards the hut and knocked on the door.

The door opened and Nang Srichaka poked her pretty head out to see who had come to visit her, only to discover it was Chownoi Tao.

"It's you!" she screamed and slammed the door on his face. "Go away and don't come near me. I find you dirty and my skin crawls at the sight of you."

Chownoi Tao was hurt and kept out of her sight the entire day. He made friends with the frogs and the fishes in the pond and told them about life as a man. Even the birds and the butterflies were fascinated by his stories and they stopped to sit on the lotus leaves to listen to him.

Nang Srichaka did not come out of the hut, but the following day she was so hungry that she decided to go to the palace kitchen and ask the cook for some food. When she went there, the cook informed her that the king had given strict instructions that food should not be given to her unless her husband accompanied her. The princess was so humiliated that she ran back to Nong Tao in tears. She thought it was better to die of starvation than ask Chownoi Tao to accompany her.

Chownoi Tao had a soft heart and could not bear to see her cry. Knowing that she did not want to look at him, he told his friend the bird to go and ask her what the problem was. The little mynah perched on the windowsill of the hut and asked, "Why is the princess sad?"

Nang Srichaka looked up and sobbed, "It would be better that I were dead. My parents have abandoned me and even the cook refuses to give me any food."

"Don't cry princess," the mynah consoled. "I'll be back in a moment." Saying that the bird flew back to the pond and told Chownoi Tao what had happened.

Taking the names of all the delicacies he could think of, Chownoi Tao produced a basketful of steaming hot food and all kinds of fruit.

"Go, my friend. Take it to my wife but don't let her know I sent it," Chownoi Tao cautioned.

It took a dozen birds to lift the basket in the air and take it to Nang Srichaka.

When she saw the basket, her face lit up and after thanking the birds, ate to her heart's content.

"Where did you get all this from?" she asked.

"Our friend who is a prince told us to deliver it to you," the mynah replied. Nang Srichaka was thoughtful. If only she had married a real prince instead of that awful creature. She wondered who the prince might be.

"Will your prince be kind enough to send me a basket of food everyday?" she asked hopefully.

"I'm certain he would not mind," the mynah replied. "After all he has the biggest heart in the entire world."

Nang Srichaka was happy to hear that. She waited for the birds to come each morning and ate whatever she fancied from the assortment of food and left the rest for the remainder of the day. Since she had no responsibilities she idled away her time walking around the garden or peeking over the fence to see what was happening in the palace. She had not visited her parents in months and she had no intention of doing so in the near future, because her father had said he would only allow her in, if she brought her husband along.

The princess soon began to tire of being on her own. She could not think of anywhere she could go to. When the birds came with the food basket in the morning she said, "I would like to meet your prince and thank him personally for being so kind." The birds told her that they would tell him to come and meet her at Nong Tao.

When Nang Srichaka went to the pond the next day, the birds sang to announce the arrival of the prince. She looked around but there was no prince in sight. All that she saw was the turtle coming out of the water towards her.

"Where is he?" she asked impatiently, looking up at the birds perched on the braches overhead.

"Are you blind princess? Don't you recognize your own husband?" the birds twittered.

"No!" she screamed. "It cannot be. You lie!" The birds fell silent. Chownoi Tao stopped in his tracks. Nang Srichaka ran blindly to her hut and locked herself in. She did not know what to

Nang Srichaka knelt down and touched Chownoi Tao's hard shell. "Forgive me, your Majesty. I have wronged you greatly." She meant every word she said.

think. Her mind was in turmoil.

Back in the palace, the king's heart began to thaw. He sent one of his slaves to enquire about his daughter's well being. When the slave arrived, she saw Nang Srichaka weeping, so she quickly went back and reported the matter to the king. He began to regret his harsh treatment towards his daughter and sent the queen to bring her home. The queen was overjoyed. She had not been happy with her husband's decision to send their daughter to live at Nong Tao and had spent sleepless nights over it. Although Nong Tao was next door to the palace, the king had forbidden anyone including the queen to go there. The queen hurried to the little hut and pushed open the door to see her daughter sitting in the corner of the room, looking very lost and lonely. It was more than her heart could bear.

"Come my child, let us go home," she said, hugging her daughter. "Your father is no longer angry with you."

Chownoi Tao was having a leisurely swim when he saw the queen and Nang Srichaka emerge from the hut and walk towards the palace. They did not even look towards the pond. He followed them, but by the time he had reached the gate, they had already disappeared from view. Chownoi Tao waited for his wife to return to Nong Tao but when darkness came and there was no sign of her, he began to fear she would never return.

Having been condemned to live in the form of a turtle was punishment enough, but knowing that he had Nang Srichaka as a companion made his existence a little easier. It was another matter that she never spoke to him or showed any sign of ever wanting to, but seeing her around was enough to lift his spirits. Now that she was gone, he found he had no reason to live. Chownoi Tao's friends tried to cheer him up, but he was inconsolable.

The princess was glad to be back in the comforts of the palace but she also felt guilty for having been so cruel to Chownoi Tao, who on the contrary had always been kind and generous. As the days passed, she wondered what Chownoi Tao was doing. After all, it was her fault that he was forever doomed to remain a turtle and live in the pond. Had it not been for her, he would have been living the life of a prince.

Nang Srichaka could not bear it any longer. She ran back to Nong Tao and called out, "Chownoi Tao! Chownoi Tao! Where are you?"

The turtle stuck its head out of the water and slowly came out. Nang Srichaka knelt down and touched Chownoi Tao's hard shell. "Forgive me, your Majesty. I have wronged you greatly." She meant every word she said.

The very next moment the turtle changed back to his human form. The spell was now broken, for Nang Srichaka had learnt to love irrespective of the person's appearance.

There was great rejoicing at the happy turn of events. The king invited the prince and his daughter to live in the palace, but the two preferred to remain at Nong Tao among their friends, the birds, butterflies and frogs.

Nong Tao: Turtle pond

21

Chow Ai and the Phephai

Chow Ai was a happy-go-lucky man who loved nothing better than to lie down by the fireplace, smoking his opium pipe. He and his wife lived in a house that was on the verge of collapse. Every time it rained, the thatch roof leaked and the water seeped in. As a result the walls and the floor of the house were in tatters.

"What a lazy husband I have. He can't even be bothered to repair the house," the wife cursed him every time her foot sank through the rotten floor. How she longed to live in a proper home with smooth shining floors and a thick pile of thatch over their heads to protect them from the incessant rains.

She toiled hard to keep the granary well stocked with grain for the entire year and always kept a ready supply of firewood piled high beneath her home. If it were possible for her to build a new house, she would have done it, but that was a man's job. As it were, the poor woman was so overburdened with work, she had no time to think pleasant thoughts and therefore no time to laugh. She turned into a bitter and resentful nag over the years. Had it not been for his wife's constant nagging Chow Ai would have been content living a lazy man's existence. When all else failed, she threatened to leave for her father's home if he did not build her a new house.

"Go and get the bamboo today!" she screamed at him for the umpteenth time as he sat curled up on the grimy mattress by the fireplace smoking his opium pipe. Tired of her nagging, he finally decided to do her bidding. "Be quiet! Instead of nagging all day get my lunch ready if you want me to get your bamboo," he said authoritatively. She quickly obeyed him lest he change his mind.

He picked up his precious pipe, his brass plate, bamboo chopsticks, brass ladle, a tuft of dried shredded banana leaves and a ball of opium. All these he lovingly packed into a cloth bag along with a ball of cooked rice and boiled vegetables wrapped in plantain leaves. With bag and mit slung over his shoulder, Chow Ai made his way into the forest. His wife heaved a sigh of relief as she watched him go.

It was a bright sunny morning and Chow Ai had to walk a long way through the dense forest before he came to the part where bamboo was found in abundance. Birds chirped in the branches overhead and flew noisily away when he took out his mit and began hacking at the bamboo. It was tough work especially for someone who was used to the easy life.

"Why can't my wife be satisfied with the house we live in," he grumbled loudly. "It's perfectly alright. Perhaps just a bit leaky but nothing to bother about."

It was already evening by the time his work was done. He could imagine his wife beaming with happiness. *There's enough bamboo here for her majesty to build a palace if she wants to.*

All that work had exhausted him completely. He sat down under the shade of a tree and after a while got down to eating his frugal meal. Never having worked that hard before, Chow Ai was so hungry he polished off every single grain of rice and every bit of vegetable that his wife had packed for him. Then he lit a fire with some dry twigs and got down to his favourite pastime. Out came the brass ladle, pipe, chopsticks, plate and ingredients from his cloth bag. He smiled contentedly and hummed a happy tune.

"Ha! Ha! What have we here?" a loud voice boomed from behind. Chow Ai turned to look back and his blood froze. A monstrous Phephai with a wicked grin was slowly lumbering towards him. He stood over ten feet tall and had prominent yellow fangs that prevented his thick lipped mouth from closing. His hair was wooly from never having been washed and he smelled like a wild beast. Looking at him was enough to make a grown man shiver.

"My luck seems to be good today. It's been a long while since I've eaten a man," the Phephai said as he made to grab hold of the unfortunate Chow Ai.

I'm done for. He's going to eat me! Chow Ai feverishly tried to think of some means of escape.

"These are your grandfather's shin bones," he said nonchalantly, wagging them at the Phephai.

"Wait!" he cried, "How can you think of eating me when I've yet to have my smoke? I was about to prepare it when you came along."

The Phephai was puzzled. He had never seen a man having a smoke before. Indeed, his curiosity got the better of him. He looked long and hard at the little fellow in front of him before making up his mind.

"Alright! Go ahead and have your smoke. After that I'm going to eat you up," he said. He might just as well have some entertainment before making a meal of the man.

The Phephai stood and watched Chow Ai as he prepared his smoke. He saw him place a dark brown ball on the ladle over the fire and stir it continuously with the chopsticks till it turned into a sticky mass. He watched curiously as Chow Ai took the ladle off the fire and keep it aside. Then he sat on his haunches and watched with great intent as Chow Ai roasted the dried shredded banana leaves on a brass plate. Chow Ai did it all very slowly so that he could buy more time. The Phephai on his part was getting more and more perplexed and impatient watching Chow Ai. Finally he could not contain his curiosity any longer.

"What is this? And that? And that? And that? And that?" the Phephai pointed a huge grubby finger at each and every article used in preparing this mysterious smoke. Chow Ai was beginning to enjoy all the attention he was getting from the Phephai. The Phephai's ignorance made him lose some of his fear. It made him think more clearly. He lifted the chopsticks for the Phephai to see.

"These are your grandfather's shin bones," he said nonchalantly, wagging them at the Phephai.

The Phephai was taken aback. He knitted his brows and took a closer look at the ivory coloured chopsticks in the man's hand. This was the first time he ever saw a Phephai's shin bone. Chow Ai decided to push his luck further.

"This is your grandfather's skull," he said tapping the brass plate with the chopsticks. "And that is your grandfather's hair," he said as he jabbed and lifted strands of the shredded banana leaves. The Phephai's eyes grew round like saucers and his mouth hung open with shock and surprise.

"This here is your grandfather's thigh bone," Chow Ai went on, pointing to the ladle "And that thing on it is your grandfather's blood," he said, sticking the chopsticks into the gooey mass of cooked opium.

Emboldened by the look of fear on the Phephai's face, Chow Ai stood up and rubbing his palms together said, "This is the last drop of your grandfather's blood and the last of his hair. What shall I eat after that? Am I not the luckiest man in the world? You show up just as I was about to finish what little was left of your grandfather. I shall have to kill you or I will die of hunger." He stood up waving the chopsticks in front of the Phephai's face, carried away by his own dramatic skills.

The Phephai trembled with fear. No Phephai had ever been able to match his grandfather in strength for he was the strongest of them all. If what this man said was true, he was in big trouble. Anyone who could kill and eat his grandfather was unquestionably invincible. He dare not do or say anything to annoy him.

"Please...please spare me," the Phephai pleaded with folded hands. "Ask me for anything you want.."

Chow Ai was a shrewd man. "What will you give me in return for letting you go?" he asked, while taking a long satisfying drag from his pipe.

The Phephai's face paled in horror as he watched his grandfather's hair and blood gurgle and turn to smoke. He quickly took off a huge gold ring from his finger and handed it to Chow Ai.

"Take this. It's a magic ring that will take you anywhere you wish to go. Just spare me," the Phephai pleaded.

Chow Ai pretended to hesitate for a moment before accepting the ring. "This ring better work or I'll find you," he said.

"It will," the Phephai promised. "I swear on my grandfather that this ring is a magic ring. Here! I'll prove it to you." The

Phephai uttered some magic words that took them flying at lightning speed to the mountain peak. Chow Ai became a little nervous for he was in unfamiliar territory.

"Take me back to the jungle," He commanded. "I have to collect my bamboo or my wife will nag me to death." The Phephai took him back to the jungle and there taught him the magic words that would transport him to any destination he so desired. Chow Ai collected his bamboo and wished himself back home. No sooner had he made his wish than he found himself in front of his home, bamboo and all. His wife almost fainted from shock when she saw him and the bamboo materialize out of thin air.

He built a beautiful house with woven bamboo strips and roofed it with a thick pile of straw. The floors gleamed to the satisfaction of his wife and she invited the whole village to a house warming party that lasted till the next morning. Both husband and wife travelled far and wide with the help of his magic ring. They had a lot of interesting stories to tell their friends and neighbours every time they returned home from their travels.

With his wife the envy of all her friends, she had nothing to complain about and Chow Ai could spend his time comfortably stretched out on his mattress engaged in his favourite pastime.

Phephai: Ogre/demon

22

The Golden Tree

The lush green forests of the Nam Yun valley was once upon a time, a virtual paradise on earth. The Khamtis had made it their home. Food was aplenty and the sound of childrens laughter echoed throughout the valley.

Their peaceful world was shattered with the arrival of an enormous bird, the likes of which was alien to the land. Inhabitants reported sightings of the monstrous bird as it tried to perch on the trees in the Nam Yun valley. Each time the bird attempted to land on the branch of a tree, the entire tree would come crashing down. This made the bird screech loudly and flap its giant wings frantically in a bid to fly away. The sound of crashing trees and the blood curdling cries of the bird sent shivers down the spine of those that heard them. After many failed attempts, the monster ultimately found a rock that was large enough to support its colossal weight.

Curious villagers flocked to have a glimpse of the giant bird wondering what kind of beast it was that had wandered into their land. They stared openmouthed as it circled the skies, casting its evil shadow on the ground. Then one day the bird lifted a child off the ground and flew towards the rock where it devoured the child. The villagers were too stunned to react and even if they did, it was to run away in fear. What chance did they have against this monstrous creature?

From then onwards, the gigantic bird would haunt the Nam Yun valley on a regular basis to prey on the children. Soon the bones of innocent children were strewn across the valley as a grim

It almost seemed as if the Gods were out to punish the inhabitants of Nam Yun by unleashing this monster upon them.

reminder of the loathsome creature.

Inspite of all the precautions taken by the villagers to safeguard their children, the bird always managed to outwit them. It grew bolder and bolder, hunting for children from their very homes till life in the valley of Nam Yun came to a standstill. People huddled within the safety of their homes, not knowing who would be the next victim.

One brave man decided to do something about it. "We cannot live in hiding for the rest of our lives," he said. "We have to fight back. Are we not real men that we cannot protect our children from danger?"

Summing up their courage the whole country took up arms

against the bird, determined to make the valley safe once more. Able men from all the villages came forward and began hunting for the bird in earnest. Any sighting of the bird was reported and hunters immediately set out to kill it. All this exercise only managed to make the bird more cautious and cunning. No matter how hard they tried, the people were unsuccessful in their attempts to kill the bird. It almost seemed as if the gods were out to punish the inhabitants of Nam Yun by having unleashed this monster upon them.

Sensing danger, the bird flew towards the hills overlooking the Nam Yun valley, searching for a convenient hideout. High up in Noi Kham in the centre of an enchanted lake, there grew an enormous tree with branches of gold and silver. The Khamtis had for centuries held the tree as sacred and worshipped it. It was on this tree that the bird found shelter, for when it descended on the topmost branches of the golden tree it discovered that the tree was strong enough to support its weight. No other tree in the land had branches that could bear the weight of this bird.

The Khamtis got together and deliberating for days on end made a grave decision. They decided to sacrifice the golden tree so that the bird would have no hiding place and it would be simpler for them to track it down in open country. With the demolition of its only sanctuary, the bird was in a quandary. It flew here and there, trying to find a tree to rest on, but every tree it perched on gave way under its weight. After being hunted for days, the tired bird perched on the rock that used to be its previous haunt. A group of four slaves having seeing it, took careful aim and let fly a volley of arrows, which pierced the bird and killed it.

The jubilant slaves were joined by men, women and children who came from far and wide to have a close look at the monster that had wrecked havoc on them. They piled dry sticks over the carcass and burned it so that no trace of it would be left behind. All that was left were the claw marks of the bird on the rock. The country was now rid of the monster and children were once more free to roam the valley in peace.

After the tree was cut down, the waters of the lake rose up

and swallowed its remains until there was no trace of the once majestic tree. Over a period of time, the lake became overgrown with weeds and in the winter when the water dried up, the weeds caught fire on their own. Every monsoon the lake at Noi Kham fills up with water and every winter the weeds mysteriously catch fire.

Noi Kham: Mountain of gold

23

How the Tiger Got its Stripes

There was a time when Tiger was Phanthoi's friend. The two shared many adventures together. Most of the time though, Phanthoi the conman always managed to make a fool out of Tiger.

The two friends were out for a walk on a very cloudy day, when Phanthoi raised an alarm. "The earth and the skies are about to meet," he shouted. "The heavens are going to fall. Quick! Let me cover you up and save you."

Tiger looked at the skies and then at the ground. The clouds were so low it did seem most likely that the two were about to collide.

"Lie down in the ditch," suggested Phanthoi, pointing to the ditch ahead. Tiger quickly jumped into the ditch and lay down with his tail in the air. Phanthoi ran over to a haystack in the nearby field and grabbed a huge bundle of hay. He spread the hay over Tiger until Tiger was completely covered. After that he fetched water and sprinkled it over the hay.

"It's raining. Can you feel the rain?" Phanthoi asked, putting his ears close to the hay.

A few drops of water seeped in through the hay and Tiger yelled back, "Yes! I can feel the rain."

Phanthoi added more hay over Tiger. He sprinkled more water and asked, "Do you still feel the rain?"

"Yes!" Tiger replied, wondering if the skies had actually collided with the earth. *I hope I'm safe,* he thought to himself.

too. "Do you still feel the rain?" he asked sweetly.

"No!" Tiger finally said.

Phanthoi set fire to the hay. "Are you feeling the heat, friend Tiger?" he called out.

The pile of hay shook violently and Tiger sprang out, moaning in sheer agony. He ran as far away as he could from the burning hay and bumped into a herd of water buffaloes lazing around on the river bank.

"Help me!" Tiger cried out to them, thrashing about on the grass. The water buffaloes took pity on him and said, "First soak yourself in the mud and then bask in the sun afterwards."

Tiger followed their advice. He rolled around till he was all covered in mud and lay down to dry himself in the sun. It worked. The pain was so much more tolerable. Tiger went to the river to wash the mud off and almost jumped out of his skin when he saw a strange striped Tiger staring back at him in the water.

"Who is that?" he growled. The water buffaloes laughed at him. "Don't you recognize your own face?" they said.

"What happened to me?" Tiger asked. "Where did I get these stripes from?"

"Those are the marks of the straw that were on your body when you got burnt," the water buffaloes explained. Tiger didn't know whether he liked himself in stripes or without them.

"I shall catch Phanthoi some day and when I do, he'll be very, very sorry," Tiger vowed. At least the pain was gone, thanks to the advice of the water buffaloes. He was extremely grateful.

Tiger followed their advice. He rolled around till he was all covered in mud and lay down to dry himself in the sun.

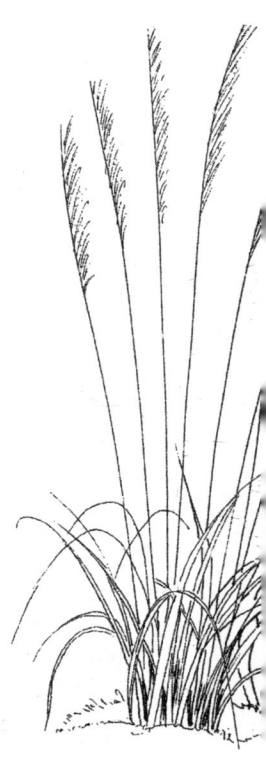

"Thank you friends," he said to the water buffaloes. "I feel much better already."

"That is our secret of relaxing ourselves after a hard day's work," said the water buffaloes.

"I promise not to hunt you at the beginning or the end of each year as a token of my gratitude," Tiger promised as he strolled away to find Phanthoi.

From then onwards it is a known fact that tigers rarely kill water buffaloes because Tiger had given them his word.

Phanthoi: Cheat/rogue

24

Chow Pingya & Nang Samati

Long, long ago, when the Nanchows waged war on other nations, there lived two brothers in the prosperous seaside town of Namchik. They were left orphaned at a young age and Chow Pingya, the elder of the two, took it upon himself to bring up his younger brother Chow Supin. Chow Pingya amassed a sizeable fortune through trade and because he was absent from home for long periods, was over indulgent with his brother who thought nothing of squandering his brother's hard earned money.

Chow Pingya married the charming Nang Samati whom he dearly loved with all his heart. Even before they could enjoy their life together as man and wife, Chow Pingya had to travel across the seas on urgent business. He would be gone for months or maybe a year, so before leaving they wept and promised to always love and be true to each other. With a heart as heavy as stone Chow Pingya set off on his journey. Not very long after his departure, Nang Samati received tragic news that her husband had drowned in a shipwreck. She wept bitterly for days till there was not a drop of tear left to be shed.

Chow Supin was now the master of the house. He approached his widowed sister-in-law with a marriage proposal, promising to love and protect her as his brother did, but Nang Samati rejected his proposal. This angered him and he struck her so hard that she fell unconscious. He tried his best to revive her but when he failed to do so he panicked and threw her into the river. Nang Samati did not die. She regained her senses and walked for many days through thick forest until she came to a road where she rested under the shade of a tree. A merchant and his wife who happened to pass by stopped to talk to her. When Nang Samati told them she had nowhere to go, they took her to the city to live with them for as long as she desired. The couple had a little child who became very attached to Nang Samati.

The servant of the house resented the way his employers placed all their trust on Nang Samati. His heart burned with jealous thoughts. *They treat her as though she is a member of the family, whereas I who have worked here for so long am not trusted.*

One warm afternoon, Nang Samati fell asleep with the baby by her side. This was the perfect opportunity that the servant had been waiting for. He quietly slipped into the room with a poisonous snake and caused it to bite the sleeping child. When the merchant and his wife returned home, the servant went crying to them, accusing Nang Samati of having killed their child.

Nang Samati pleaded her innocence but the distraught parents ordered her to leave at once. When she saw the triumphant look on the servant's face she realized that he was somehow responsible for the baby's death.

Nang Samati walked out of the house not knowing where to go. While on her way, she was accosted by a robber who snatched her belongings. Finding nothing of value, he sold her off to a slave merchant who put her on board a ship about to set sail. There were other slaves on board but they were all men. Seeing that she was the only woman on board, Nang Samati prayed to God for help. A miracle took place whereby she was physically transformed into a man and thereafter known as Chow Sa. After many months of sailing, the ship dropped anchor on foreign shores.

It so happened that the king of that country had died without leaving an heir and it was left to the ceremonial horse with divine powers to find a new king. When Chow Sa walked down the ship's plank, the ceremonial horse reared up and neighed, as if saluting him. People rushed forward, helped him onto the horse and led him through the city in a joyous procession. The courtiers arranged a grand ceremony where they crowned him king. In the years that followed, Chow Sa proved to be a very capable ruler and was respected and loved by his subjects. He was greatly inclined towards meditation and prayers and possessed healing powers.

One day while Chow Sa was touring his kingdom, he saw a blind beggar being teased by some children. He immediately ordered his guards to bring the beggar to him. "May the Gods bless you and restore your sight," he told the beggar.

The very next moment the beggar shouted, "I can see! I can see! God bless the king, for he has cured me." He fell at the feet of the king and thanked him profusely. Chow Sa's reputation as a healer spread far and wide. Blind people came flocking from across the seas and went back cured and jubilant.

After many months of sailing, the ship dropped anchor on foreign shores.

Meanwhile, Chow Pingya who had been given up for dead was very much alive. He had managed to cling to a piece of driftwood and was picked up by a passing ship. Chow Pingya travelled to many countries before boarding a ship that brought him back to his hometown.

Upon his arrival, he discovered that things were not the same. His brother had turned blind and his beloved wife was missing. Chow Pingya was heartbroken. He went from place to place enquiring about his wife. Everywhere he drew a blank. No one had ever seen her or heard of her before. He was slowly losing hope of ever finding her again. During one of his journeys he saw two blind men on the wayside and feeling sorry for them, took them home. Chow Pingya had heard stories of the king who could cure the blind and he decided to take his brother and the two men to be cured.

One day Chow Sa was informed that a merchant by the name of Chow Pingya of Namchik and three blind men were seeking an audience with him. He recognized Chow Pingya as soon as he saw him enter the court, even though many years had elapsed. Chow Pingya came forward and bowing to the king, introduced himself and the three blind men with him.

"Your Highness!" he said. "I have heard that you can cure the blind, so I have brought them all the way from Namchik."

Chow Sa recognized all the three blind men for they were the ones who had harmed him a long time ago. He promised to help them on condition that they confess their crimes.

The first one confessed. "I had kidnapped a girl and sold her to a merchant in exchange for a bag of silver. From then onwards I have not not been able to see. I realized God had punished me for my actions."

Chow Sa placed his hands over the robber's eyes and said, "You have done great wrong, but since you have confessed, your sight will be restored." As soon as he said that, the robber could feel a curtain being lifted from his eyes and he cried with happiness at being able to see again.

Having witnessed the miracle happen to the robber, the servant spoke. "I killed my master's child and put the blame on a woman who was innocent. My master believed me and sent the woman away. I lost my sight that day itself and have regretted my actions ever since."

Chow Sa placed his hands over the servant's eyes and said, "Your master may not forgive you for your crime, but I will restore your sight since you have spoken the truth." The servant was able to see again. He fell at the feet of the king and wept with happiness and gratitude.

Chow Pingya held his brother's hand. "Come brother, open your heart to the king. He has cured the other two and he will cure you too." Chow Supin however refused to speak. He turned to leave.

"Stop! I command you to tell me everything. Now!" Chow Sa ordered.

Finding no way out, Chow Supin confessed, "I was told my brother was dead so I proposed to my widowed sister-in-law. When she rejected my proposal, I was so angry, I hit her and killed her accidently. I didn't mean to kill her. After I disposed off her body in the river, I lost my sight."

Chow Pingya was stunned on hearing his brother's confession. It was something he could never have imagined. His world came crashing down now that his wife's death was confirmed.

Placing his hand over the eyes of Chow Supin, Chow Sa said, "What you did was wrong, but because you have confessed, you are henceforth cured." Chow Supin's happiness at being able to see again was marred by the fact that he could not bear to look at his brother's face out of shame.

Chow Pingya returned to his ship with a heavy heart. He was deeply hurt by his brother's betrayal. As he sat alone on the deck thinking of the day's events, a messenger came up to him and handed him a box wrapped in silk. It contained a set of royal garments and a bejeweled sword.

"The king desires that you meet him tomorrow morning," the messenger said. Chow Pingya was puzzled. *Why has the king sent me these gifts? Why does he want to meet me?*

Next morning Chow Pingya went to the palace dressed in the garments presented to him. The king greeted him warmly and made him comfortable. As they got talking, the king asked him if he was married.

"I was married once but my wife is no more," Chow Pingya replied.

"What if your wife is still alive?" the king asked.

"If she is still alive, I would take her home," Chow Pingya replied. "But, my brother's confession has killed all hope that she may be alive."

"Would you remember your wife after all these years?" the king was curious to know.

"I would recognize her by her touch," Chow Pingya replied without hesitation.

"Well then," the king said. "Be here tomorrow. I have a surprise for you."

Chow Pingya went back to his ship wondering what surprise the king had in store for him. *Could my wife still be alive? No! I dare not hope for such a thing and yet why was the king so curious to know about my past? Does he know something about Nang Samati?*

The next day the king prepared his courtiers for what was to come. "Chow Pingya is a noble person. His character towers over most men, including mine. Would you be happy if he were to sit on this throne as king?" He asked.

The courtiers were surprised hearing this from their king. Then one of them spoke, "If your Majesty feels he is superior to you, we would consider ourselves very fortunate to have him as king. However, we already have you as our king and we are happy under your rule."

The king was silent for a while before speaking. "I support him for a reason. Listen then, to my story..." and the king related his entire life history to his courtiers, ending his story with, "I shall now ask the Gods to grant me back my true form."

The king sat in deep meditation and before the eyes of his astonished courtiers morphed into a beautiful woman. Nang Samati immediately sent for Chow Pingya.

Ninety slaves were made to stand behind a line of silk screens with Nang Samati among them. When Chow Pingya arrived he was led inside and asked to see if he could recognize his wife by just holding her hands. All the ninety slaves standing behind the screens including Nang Samati stuck out their palm. Chow Pingya moved from one screen to the next, touching each palm. "No, this is not it," he kept saying, until he held Nang Samati's hand. There was an instant connection.

"Is it you my dear wife? No, it cannot be, for you are dead," Chow Pingya cried out in anguish, holding tightly on to her hands.

He could hear sobbing from the other side of the screen. Attendants removed the screen and the two came face to face with one another and were reunited. Their search had finally come to an end.

The news spread like the wind across the kingdom and people flocked to see their king who had now turned into a woman. Amid great pomp and splendour, Chow Pingya and Nang Samati were crowned king and queen. The brother-in-law, Chow Supin, the robber and the servant recognized the face of the queen and came to ask for forgiveness. Nang Samati readily forgave them for she felt they were punished enough.

Chow Pingya and Nang Samati ruled wisely and lived the rest of their lives in great happiness.

25

The Manang Tree

Chow Ngee, a poor farmer had just finished work and was on his way home from the paddy fields. The sun was about to set so he took the shorter route home. On the way he came across a man who was sitting under a shady manang tree, scratching his head vigorously as though it was infested with lice. The branches of the manang tree were high and were laden with ripe fruit. Chow Ngee wanted to pluck some of the fruit for his wife.

Noticing him looking up at the fruit, the man spoke to Chow Ngee. "If you want to eat it you'll have to climb up the tree."

"That's exactly what I was thinking about," Chow Ngee replied. Gathering up the hem of his fanoy, he swung it under his legs and tucked it behind the waist into a swaddle. He then grasped hold of the trunk and slowly made his way up the tree like a seasoned climber. Settling down on a sturdy branch, he stretched out to pluck the fruit and let it drop to the ground.

"Be careful when you drop the manang. See that it doesn't fall on me," the man below cautioned.

Chow Ngee looked down for a moment and almost fell off the branch in shock at what he saw. The man had removed his scalp and had spread it over his bended knee. Chow Ngee's heart thumped loudly as he watched the man meticulously part the hair on his scalp looking for lice. The man plucked out the lice and killed them between his thumbnails, shouting with glee every time he did that. Chow Ngee quivered with fright and the manang fell out of his grasp and landed with a mighty plop right in the middle of the exposed skull.

The sour juice of the manang burned the puhsu's open skull and he howled in agony. Arranging his scalp back into place, the puhsu looked up at Chow Ngee, his eyes flashing in anger. "So you've discovered my secret. I will have to kill you now!" He stood up and held the tree.

"Manang tree, I command you to bend." The tree swayed and bent down almost touching the ground.

"Manang tree...UP!" Chow Ngee shouted anxiously as he clutched the branch for dear life. The tree jerked up and Chow Ngee felt safe, but not for long.

"Manang tree...bend..bend.." the puhsu shouted from below. The tree obeyed and bent down. The puhsu almost caught hold of Chow Ngee before he shouted, "Manang tree..up...UP!"

This went on for a while. The tree bent down to the command of the puhsu and jerked up at Chow Ngee's request. Up and down it went, until poor Chow Ngee's head began to spin and his concentration wavered. In his confused state he shouted "Manang tree..bend..bend.." The tree stayed bent on the ground and the puhsu managed to catch hold of Chow Ngee and plucked him off his perch.

The unfortunate Chow Ngee was now at the mercy of the puhsu who was in no mood to spare him. Crazed with fear, Chow Ngee saw the puhsu's face distort and stretch to double its normal length with a tongue that resembled a snake. He had vaguely heard of such things before but had never believed them to be true. Chow Ngee mercifully blanked out after a severe beating. Leaving him for dead, the puhsu went deep into the forest to look for his wife so that they could feast together on the fallen victim.

Battered and bruised, Chow Ngee regained consciousness after a while. He crawled away into the jungle and did not stop until he came to an abandoned hut. Not wanting to take any chances, he climbed up the rafters and lay hidden under the thatch roof. Feeling hungry he took out a manang from inside his shirt and was just about to take a bite when he heard strange sounds. It turned out to be a group of puhsus carrying an unconscious man

"Manang tree, I command you to bend." The tree swayed and bent down almost touching the ground.

inside a huge golden pot and a sack of gold and silver dishes. After lighting a fire they put water in the pot to boil and danced around their victim, shouting so loudly that the man woke up.

Chow Ngee realized they intended to boil the poor man and eat him right under his nose. The thought of it make him shiver so violently that the manang slipped out of his fingers and fell down. At that very instant there was a loud clap of thunder. The manang fell with a loud plop into the pot, splashing water all about just as thunder and lightening crashed and lit up the little hut.

"The Gods are angry with us!" the puhsus screamed in alarm. "Quick! Let's get out before we're all killed." They ran out of the hut in a great hurry leaving all their gold utensils behind. After they had gone and everything was quiet, Chow Ngee jumped down and tapped the terrified man on the shoulder. "Hurry up and follow me if you want to escape."

They emptied the golden pot and filled it with the gold and silver dishes. Holding the pot by the handles they both hurried out into the pouring rain. There was no sight of any puhsus. The two men reached Chow Ngee's home safely, much to the relief of his wife and sister. The man was very grateful to Chow Ngee for having saved him from the jaws of death. He married Chow Ngee's sister and after selling off the golden vessels they all had enough money to live a comfortable life.

Manang: Very sour fruit; Fanoy: Lungi/gent's tartan skirt; Puhsu: Witch/wizard

26

Mok Phet the Liar

In the good old days when the Nanchows were at war, there lived a man by the name of Mok Phet. That wasn't his real name, but one he had acquired because of his talent for telling lies.

One fine day, Mok Phet was taking a leisurely stroll along the river bank when a girl stopped to talk to him. She neatly balanced six waterpots on her head and made quite an impressive picture.

"I hear you are a famous liar. Come, try and see if you can lie to me," she challenged. Mok Phet looked at her and found her to be quite gullible.

"Not now, maybe later, the sun has risen from the opposite direction today and I'm on my way to tell the king about it. I really must rush."

The girl's immediate reaction was to look up, causing the water pots to topple over. She stood open mouthed in the middle of a large puddle of water and bits of broken clay, knowing she had been fooled.

She wasn't the first person in the village to fall for his lies and certainly not the last either. There soon came a time when the people in the village felt they had had enough and decided to teach him a lesson. They caught him and took him to the river bank where they tied him up with stout ropes. As darkness approached, everybody left for their homes and Mok Phet was left sitting where he was.

He spied a fisherman rowing his boat down river and shouted

She stood open mouthed in the middle of a large puddle of water and bits of broken clay, knowing she had been fooled.

for help. Steering his boat closer to the bank, the fisherman saw Mok Phet thrashing about on the grass.

"What are you doing here?" the fisherman asked. "Who tied you up?"

"Thieves broke into my house and left me here after robbing all my money," Mok Phet replied. Feeling sorry for him, the fisherman untied him. He even gave him a couple of fish to take home before moving on. Mok Phet went home and cooked himself a tasty dish of fish and rice for dinner.

The next day when the villagers saw him they were amazed. "How did you manage to return home?" they asked. "Who set you free?"

Smooth talker that he was, Mok Phet began his tale. "Well, after you all left me, I dozed off and fell into the river. A beautiful water nymph came and untied me. She led me to a place where the water God stores all his treasures. There were heaps and heaps of gold and silver articles in the deep end. Unfortunately I had fallen into the shallow end so I was given only fish. If I had fallen into the deep end I would have been showered with so much riches that I would not have known what to do."

"How do you expect us to believe you? They asked. "You're always lying. Show us some proof."

Mok Phet went in and brought out a pot filled with fish bones. They marvelled at his stroke of good luck.

Taking advantage of the situation Mok Phet convinced them to have themselves tied up and thrown into the deep end of the river. The women cheered him on as he pushed their husbands from the boat. They waited for their husbands to return home that night, and when there was no sign of any of them the next morning, the women went to Mok Phet.

"How is it that our husbands are not back as yet?" they asked.

"Perhaps the water nymphs have taken them to the water God's palace," Mok Phet replied. "You'll have to wait because there'll be so much treasure there that they'll take time to choose what to carry back."

The foolish women went home satisfied with what they were told. They waited and waited and if your guess is as good as mine, they're still waiting for their husbands to come home loaded with riches.

Mok Phet: Habitual liar

27

Chow Dhammasethe

Long, long ago, there lived a king who ruled wisely and was loved by his subjects. A son was born to him after many years and the king had great plans lined up for the little prince. Sadly, the queen passed away and the king being busy with affairs of state, had to rely on the servants for the upbringing of his son Dhammasethe. The boy had a voracious appetite for knowledge and his father satisfied his craving by employing the best teachers to tutor him.

The king's widowed sister had a son who was of the same age as the prince. When the sister remarried, she left her son Sila in the care of her brother. The king was pleased because his son would not be lonely any more. As they grew older, the king decided to send them both to Takaso, which was on the other side of the mountains, for their higher education.

Arrangements were made for the two young men at Takaso. They were to stay in the house of a merchant who regularly rented out rooms. The merchant's daughter Eleng was about ten years older than the two cousins and in those days considered an old maid. No respectable man in Takaso was willing to marry her because of her quarrelsome nature. There had been a few offers of marriage from men of poorer means but Eleng turned up her nose at them. She was an ambitious woman for whom money and status meant everything.

When Eleng saw the two young men she was elated, for they were unlike the other tenents her father normally had. She made up her mind to marry Dhammasethe when she got to know that he was a prince. Making the first move she approached the shy young prince and made it be known that she fancied him. The prince on the contrary regarded her as an elder sister and treated her respectfully. Eleng did not give up though. She made it a point to be the first one to greet him in the morning and the last one to see him off to bed at night. Her constant chatter was beginning to get on his nerves and disturbing his studies, but he was too polite to say anything that would offend her. Eleng on the other hand was becoming impatient. Inspite of all the attention she showered on him, the prince did not reciprocate her feelings. She bluntly told the prince that she was in love with him and wanted to marry him. The prince was horrified.

"You are like my elder sister," he exclaimed. "How can you even think of such things?"

His answer was like a blow to Eleng. Fuming inwardly and swearing revenge, Eleng shifted her attention to Sila and before long had him under her spell. Eleng kept her distance from Dhammasethe and spoke to him only when absolutely necessary.

The merchant and his wife meanwhile had always wanted a son-in-law who possessed the fine qualities that Dhammasethe had. That he was heir to the throne after his father was an added bonus. Their daughter was not getting any younger and the prince was a prize catch. They knew from the start that their daughter had a great liking for the prince and had encouraged her by giving her the freedom to spend as much time as she wanted in his company. What they did not suspect was that their daughter was carrying on a clandestine affair with Sila. So secretive were the two lovers that not even Dhammasethe had an inkling of what was happening. When the two young men had completed their education, Dhammasethe thanked the merchant and asked him if he required anything.

"I have a small request," the merchant replied.

"Whatever it is, I shall be happy to do it for you. I give you my word," Dhammasethe said.

"Accept my daughter as your wife," the merchant said. "That is my humble request."

Dhammasethe could not believe his ears. This was not something he had expected to hear. He was most reluctant to marry Eleng, but the merchant's wife prevailed upon him to accept her daughter. "We are old and will not live forever," she said tearfully. "You may keep her as a servant in your palace if you so desire, but please do us this favour by marrying our daughter."

Ultimately under tremendous pressure Dhammasethe agreed to the marriage but on condition that no guests be invited. The merchant and his wife were only too happy to agree. When Sila came to know of it he was dumbfounded and angry, but Eleng placated him with sweet words. Together they hatched a plot to get rid of Dhammasethe.

As soon as the marriage ceremony was over, Dhammasethe along with his wife and cousin took leave of his in-laws. Their journey on horseback across the mountains was long and arduous. As night fell they dismounted and retired for the night under the stars. The unsuspecting Dhammasethe was fast asleep when his treacherous cousin and wife pushed him off the high mountain into the valley below. Confident that Dhammasethe would not survive the fall, they continued their journey without any remorse and reached their destination.

Dhammasethe had landed on some bushes a great distance below and was unconscious for a while. When he opened his eyes he saw a handsome youth smiling down at him and offering him a cup of water. Dhammasethe drank the water and miraculously felt all his aches and pains vanish.

"Who are you?" he asked the stranger.

"I am the spirit of the forest and you are my guest," the stranger replied and disappeared into thin air. Dhammasethe explored the forest and found it had an abundance of fruit trees and a crystal clear stream. Over the next few days he built a hut for himself and sheltered there. It was a beautiful place and the prince was in no hurry to get back to civilization after what had happened.

The magnificent horse roamed the length and breadth of the country for days before stopping in front of the hut where Dhammasethe resided. It reared up and neighed long and loud.

The old king had long awaited the return of his son and was heartbroken when Sila returned without his son. He passed away after a few days and since there was no heir, Sila ascended the throne with Eleng as his queen. Burdened with guilt, Sila took to drinking heavily and had no time to attend to matters of state importance while his wife went on a spending spree. Eleng embarked on a reign of wasteful expenditure that drained the royal treasury. She surrounded herself with sycophants and hangers-on who distanced her from reality.

The people were disgusted with their ruler whom they never saw and who never bothered to get to know his subjects. During a celebration held at the palace, a group of actors came dressed in Phephai masks and attacked the royal couple. The king and queen called for the guards but no one came forward to their aid. The actors were joined by the disgruntled townspeople who chased the king and queen with clubs and swords deep into the forests. They were warned never to return if they valued their lives.

Since the kingdom could not remain without a ruler, the council of ministers decided to follow an old tradition. They performed a religious ceremony after which the ceremonial horse leading a procession set forth in search of the new king.

The magnificent horse roamed the length and breath of the country for days before stopping in front of the hut where Dhammasethe resided. It reared up and neighed long and loud. Dhammasethe opened the door and was greeted with garlands of flowers and loud cheers. He mounted the horse and led his men back to his kingdom where he ruled as wisely as his father had.

28
The Man Nobody Wanted

Long, long ago there lived a man by the name of Konyuk. He was born into an extremely wealthy family of merchants and led a totally pampered lifestyle. His parents gave him all that his heart desired and when they died, Konyuk spent all their hard earned money in drinking and making merry. One day his friends informed him about a poor man who had three beautiful daughters. Konyuk visited the poor man's house and was captivated by the beauty of the three comely sisters named Yaekok, Enam and Ampot. He immediately sent the customary gift of sugar, money and flowers on a silver platter through the local matchmaker. The parents happily accepted the platter, which meant that the proposal was accepted and offered their eldest daughter Yaekok in marriage to Konyuk. The matchmaker cleared his throat and made it be known that Konyuk wanted to marry all three daughters.

The poor man was shocked and reluctant to agree to such an arrangement, but his wife called him aside and said, "It will be better for our children if they all live together in one house. We are poor and we cannot provide the kind of life they will have if they marry Konyuk."

It was therefore decided that all three sisters would marry Konyuk. The marriage was conducted with great fanfare and created quite a stir for it was quite unusual even in those days for a man to marry more than one girl at a time. Konyuk would have gladly married four sisters if there had been a fourth, but the king

Konyuk visited the poor man's house and was captivated by the beauty of the three comely sisters.

had forbidden any man to have more than three wives at a time. It was the king's sole prerogative to marry as many wives as he pleased.

Konyuk settled down to a happy married life and the three sisters took no time in getting used to their new lifestyle. He was very attentive to them and gave them whatever they wanted. Anything that he bought was bought in threes so that none of them felt he favoured the other. The three sisters were the envy of friends whose husbands had little time or money for them. Their friends spoke glowingly of Konyuk to their husbands for he plied all of them with lavish gifts and profuse compliments. The women spent so much time at Konyuk's house that they began neglecting their own homes. Konyuk's wives grew jealous of the women for stealing their husbands' affection and became cold towards them. The husbands blamed Konyuk for their wives' indiscretions.

Disgusted with his ways, his neighbours, friends and relatives shut their doors and pretended not to be home when they saw him approaching. One day he fell seriously ill and realized that none of his wives cared for him.

"Yaekok! Enam! Ampot!" he called out to his wives. They heard him but did not respond, each one thinking that the other would answer his call. His servants attended to him and served him well, for Konyuk was a generous employer if not a good husband. They were the only ones who felt sorry for him. Even his relatives and so called friends did not visit him during his illness. Konyuk realized no one loved him and before he could even feel sorry for himself, he succumbed to his illness.

His wives did not mourn at his funeral and neither did they bother to make any offerings to the temple, the monks or to the poor, as was the custom. He was covered in an old white sheet and cremated. It was as if he had no family and no money. Konyuk's spirit felt utterly sad, for even though he was dead he could see and hear all that was taking place. He watched his three wives talking among themselves.

"At last our husband has found peace," Yaekok sighed.

"But I pity the Gods. They are the ones who won't have peace now that he's gone to Maung Phe." Enam laughed.

"More likely his new residence is Maung Ngalai." Ampot giggled. "Do you suppose the Phephais will have him there?"

Unable to bear the callousness of his wives, Konyuk's soul flew at tremendous speed to a place that was neither heaven nor hell. Four wise looking men, who he thought were judges, sat before him. He felt they could read his thoughts and although no one talked, they all communicated with one another telepathically.

"How have you lived your life on earth?" they asked him. Konyuk fell deep in thought. His life had been one of self indulgence, superficial friendships and time spent wastefully. It was funny how clearly he was able to see things from a different perspective, as if a veil had been lifted along with his corrupt body.

There was nothing he had done that he was proud of. He did not want to answer their question but somehow the choice was not his. He found he could not lie in front of the judges and so he told them the honest truth.

The judges deliberated over his actions and made their decision. They sentenced him to Maung Ngalai. It was only befitting that one who had committed such immoral acts be sent to the land of the Phephais. There was a feeling of dread in Konyuk's mind. He did not want to go to Maung Ngalai, after all he did not kill anyone. Yet, could he go against the decision of the judges?

Konyuk's soul went straight to Maung Ngalai. It was an extremely hot place where Phephais of all shapes and sizes with huge iron chains dragged the wicked souls around. The sound of rattling chains and screaming victims was too much for Konyuk to bear.

"Please.....let me go," he begged the fearsome Phephai who was slowly approaching him.

"What is your name?" the Phephai demanded.

"Konyuk" he replied in a small voice. At this, the Phephai let out an angry roar that made Konyuk quiver.

"You can't stay here!" the Phephai shouted indignantly. "I have four wives and I can't have you ruining my happiness."

"Most of us are married here. We don't want you coming in and creating any trouble," another Phephai shouted. Others too voiced their disapproval and in a twinkling the Phephais rushed forward and chased Konyuk out of the fiery gates. This was the first time that a condemned man was considered too risky to be kept in Maung Ngalai.

Konyuk found himself at the gates of Maung Chatu Mahalet. It was more beautiful than earth and a great change from Maung Ngalai. Konyuk was glad the Phephais had sent him to such a marvellous place. The past few hours had been a traumatic experience for him.

Oh God! I must have done something good in my life to deserve this. His heart almost exploded with sheer happiness.

The Gods of Maung Chatu Mahalet did not share his thoughts. "We can't let you in, with the kind of reputation that you have." Without giving him a chance to speak they sent him spinning to his next destination. Konyuk found himself in another heaven, even better than the one he had just been ejected from. Here too the Gods refused him entry because they wanted no disturbance to their otherwise peaceful existence. They directed him to a higher plane. Konyuk thus went from one heaven to another until he found himself outside the magnificent gates of Maung Tuksita, the world of eternal bliss.

Thoroughly demoralised, Konyuk waited for yet another rejection, but he was in for a surprise. The Gods welcomed him in without any hesitation and the moment he breathed the pure air of Maung Tuksita, Konyuk was reformed. He felt as if a heavy burden had been lifted off him and experienced pure unconditional love for the first time. Konyuk was no longer the man nobody wanted.

Maung Ngalai: Hell; Maung Phe: Paradise; Phephai: Demon; Maung Chatu Mahalet: Heaven

29

Spirit of the Mit

Chow Sye was a farmer who lived with his wife and three children in a remote village. Both he and his wife were extremely hard working and had enough to live a comfortable life. They had a roof over their heads, their granary was full and there was plenty of fresh vegetables and fruits growing in the wild. The stream running next to their house provided them fresh fish, prawns and crab.

Chow Sye's most precious possession was his mit, which was always found slung across his chest. The mit had a long and fascinating history. It had previously belonged to Chow Sye's father who was an excellent ironsmith. Having earned a good name for himself, customers came to him from afar to order their mits and swords. The king himself had come to place an order for a special sword that could slice through all kinds of metal. It was an impossible task and since the old man could not afford to displease the king he tried various methods but his efforts were in vain. He was so engrossed in trying to forge the king's sword that he put off other customers. By and by he became so poor that he was left with just enough iron to make a single sword.

One day he was so tired that he left the bits and pieces of iron on the ground to be picked up later. Unknowingly his wife scattered grain over them for the ducks. The birds gobbled up the grain along with the bits of iron. When the old man came looking for his precious metal, he was furious to discover that the ducks had eaten them up.

It was an impossible task and since the old man could not afford to displease the king he tried various methods but his efforts were in vain.

The poor wife was berated by her angry husband and told what a stupid woman she was. Desperate to rectify her mistake, she plucked some tamarind from a nearby tree and fed them to the ducks. After what seemed an eternity the ducks discharged the bits of iron, which the happy woman gathered, and gave to her husband. He forged a sword with it and when he tried it out, it exceeded his expectations. The sword did not rust and could slice through any metal. He had discovered the perfect metal because of his wife's silly mistake.

The king was so pleased with the sword that he appointed the old man master ironsmith and made him supervise the manufacture of all the royal weapons. The old man and his wife kept their formula a closely guarded secret and after his death not even his son knew what went into the making of the metal. His father however did leave him a mit if not the secret art of making it. Chow Sye wore his mit everywhere he went and had a special bond with it, treating it as if it were a living extension of himself.

The love and care that Chow Sye lavished on his mit attracted a wandering spirit looking for a home. It entered the mit, enjoyed the loving treatment from Chow Sye and vowed to repay him back by protecting him from all harm. Chow Sye noticed a sudden change in the appearance of his mit. It sparkled even when the sun hid behind dark clouds. It felt lighter than ever and was very accurate. Sometimes Chow Sye wondered if a spirit controlled his mit. He would have been shocked if he knew how close he was to the truth.

One day while returning late from a hunt, he came across a dilapidated hut where he stopped for the night. Someone had only recently been there, for the embers in the fireplace glowed a little red. Chow Sye soon had a blazing fire and went off to sleep, his mit by his side. An evil forest spirit on the prowl was attracted to the light inside the hut and stopped by, waiting for the man to sleep.

"Is anybody there?" it whispered. Chow Sye was fast asleep, but the spirit of his mit was wide awake. "Whoever it is, go away," the mit replied curtly. The evil spirit was afraid to enter for it realized there was someone more powerful inside the hut. It waited patiently outside, circling the hut but yet afraid to enter.

"Are you awake or asleep?" it whispered through the cracks in the wall. The mit at once replied, "I am awake, go away!" The evil spirit shrank back but did not leave. It could smell a man inside and it was hungry.

The fire was dying out and the cold awakened Chow Sye. Without thinking he pulled out his mit from its scabbard and prodded the embers to light the fire again. The heat of the fire killed the spirit of the mit. His mit was now lifeless and dull. Chow Sye immediately went back to sleep, not realizing the damage he had done.

The evil spirit was becoming more and more impatient. "Are you awake or asleep?" it whispered once more and upon getting no response, entered the hut and devoured the sleeping man.

It is a strong belief among the Khamtis that no mit should ever be put into the fire because fire kills the good spirit residing in it.

Mit: Machete /knife

30

Gold or Grain

In a faraway village there lived two neighbours who constantly squabbled and competed with each other. One was a farmer and the other a businessman. Both men worked very hard and were successful in their chosen field. Their children were friends but like their fathers, they too played the game of one-upmanship.

"We have a sack full of gold and silver in our house while you poor people have none," the businessman's son scoffed at the farmer's son. The farmer's son ran home to his father in tears.

"Father, are we very poor? Khamhu says we are poor because we do not have any gold or silver like them." The farmer was quick to take offence. "What does he know? Does his father know how much grain we have? If we were to compare our grain with their gold we would have a hundred times more than them." The little boy's eyes lit up and he ran to convey the message to his friend.

Khamhu took up the matter with his father as soon as the tired man got home for lunch. *How dare the farmer compare his measly grain with gold?* So annoyed was he that he immediately marched off to the farmer's house.

"I can buy off all your grain and still have more gold than you," he told the farmer who was having his dinner. The farmer took a moment to swallow his food before replying. "My grain is worth more than all your gold and silver."

"Ha! Ha! You are a strange fellow!" the businessman laughed. "Why don't we go to the king and let him settle this matter once and for all?"

"Alright!" the farmer agreed. "But his majesty will want some proof."

"That's easy," the businessman replied. "I'll take all my gold and silver and you take your grain." They decided to leave for the king's court the following day.

"How are you going to carry all the grain? We do not have enough sacks and neither do we have a cart," the farmer's wife fretted. Indeed, they had very little else besides their granary which was always full of grain. Perhaps it was not such a good idea to go to the king. The more she thought about it the more she began to worry about how her husband was going to manage this seemingly impossible task.

"What are we going to do?" she asked. "Have you thought of a solution?"

"Make me a khowpuk hat and cloak," the farmer said. "Have it ready by night time."

The obedient wife set to work at once. She went to her friend and exchanged a basket of grain for some sesame. While waiting for the rice to cook, she roasted the sesame and pounded it to a fine powder. Then she emptied the cooked rice into a large tub and sprinked salt and sesame powder over it. Both husband and wife took turns with the pestle, pounding the rice into sticky dough. They patted the dough into the shape of a conical hat and a cloak. It was already dark by the time they finished and both were totally exhausted.

The businessman did not have any problem. He simply bought a new sack and filled it with his gold and silver. When he woke up the next day he wore his best clothes, loaded the sack onto a horse drawn cart and set off for the palace. He slowed down in front of his neighbour's gate and almost fell off the cart in surprise at what he saw. The farmer seemed to be wearing something stiff and bulky and had trouble moving about.

"Do you want a ride on my cart?" the businessman shouted out. The farmer was reluctant to accept a ride from his competitor but his wife whispered, "Go! You can hardly walk in what you're wearing and it's a long journey to the king's palace."

"It looks like you are carrying the entire contents of your granary on your body," the businessman smirked.

"Only a little bit of it my friend. A tiny grain, compared to what I have at home," the farmer answered good naturedly.

After a long and tiring journey they reached the gates of the imperial palace. The guards led them into the royal court. What a strange sight they made. A well dressed man bent double under the load of a heavy sack accompanied by an oddly dressed man. The king's eyes almost popped out of his head when the two men were presented before him.

"What brings you here?" he asked.

"I can buy off all your grain and still have more gold than you," he told the farmer.

The businessman spoke first. "Your majesty," he said. "We cannot decide which one of us is richer. I have this sack full of gold and silver while he only has a granary that's full of grain. We have come all the way to meet you so that you may judge which one of us is richer."

"Fools!" the king thundered. "Do you think I have nothing better to do than make silly judgements? I'll have you thrown in prison and you can stay there till you both decide between yourselves who is richer."

The two men were taken to prison and locked up, sack and all. They had never in their wildest dreams expected the king to react in this manner.

"It's so unjust of the king to lock us up like criminals. We haven't committed any crime," the farmer grumbled. "It's all your fault. You were the one to suggest this stupid idea of coming here."

"Perhaps if you had not worn that silly costume the king might have listened to us," the businessman replied. They argued on and on till it got dark and their throats went dry.

"I'm hungry," the businessman complained. He walked to the door and yelled out, "Guards! When are we getting food? We're hungry."

"We have not been told to give you food," the guard replied and walked off to another part of the building.

"Does the king want us to starve to death?" the businessman said. "Does he think we can survive on air?"

"Luckily I won't starve," the farmer said as he broke off a piece of his hat and ate it. "My wife is an excellent cook. The salt and sesame are in just the right propotion." The businessman looked longingly at the khowpuk. His stomach growled in protest.

"Let me have a little bit of your khowpuk," he said at last. "I'm really hungry."

"Food is scarce here," the farmer replied. "If I share it with you what will be left for me to eat?"

"No! No! I don't want it for free. I'll pay you for it," the businessman said, opening his sack and taking out a silver coin.

The farmer took the coin and handed him a very tiny piece of khowpuk in return. The businessman was about to protest but he knew he could not afford to offend the farmer. Not when he depended on him for food.

"Isn't your khowpuk overpriced?" the businessman asked. "For that amount I could have bought a sack of grain."

"So why don't you do that?" the farmer replied. "I'm not forcing you to buy from me."

The businessman was hungry. The morsel of khowpuk he had eaten only served to whet his appetite. He took out a handful of coins and kept on buying pieces of khowpuk from the farmer until his stomach was full. The same thing was repeated the next day and the next until the khowpuk hat and cloak were over and there was not a crumb left. The businessman dug into his sack each time he was hungry and the farmer handed him a tiny piece of khowpuk in exchange. The farmer was now the proud owner of the sack of gold and silver that had not so long ago belonged to the businessman.

"Now who do you think is richer?" asked the farmer with a satisfied look on his face.

"You have reduced me to the status of a pauper," the businessman pointed out. "All my gold now belongs to you. If you are not rich, who is?"

The two men called the guards and said they had come to an agreement and no longer needed to be kept in jail. The king had released them and they went home, one richer and the other poorer but both undoubtedly wiser.

Khowpuk: Sticky rice cake

31

Mokmo and the Prince

The great king of Aphipataka and his queen were blessed with a son and there was great rejoicing in the land. The prince, Chow Phiwan grew up into a handsome lad more inclined towards fun than studies. Fearing that their son might turn out to be a wastrel, the king sent him abroad for studies along with the minister's son, the conscientious and intelligent Chow Kem. It was hoped that Chow Kem's company would prove beneficial to the fun loving prince.

The two boys stayed with their teacher on the outskirts of the city of Dhana and were taught everything from the arts to science, administration and warfare. Chow Phiwan was excellent in sports and swordsmanship but showed no interest in his studies, while Chow Kem emerged a brilliant scholar. Towards the end of their education, their teacher decided to test them. He handed each one a waterpot covered with a little towel.

"Wake up early and fill your pots with the Mohomahang water," he instructed. "Bring it to me after you have done so. I do not want you to discuss how you propose to get it and neither will I tell you what it is. You have to find out for yourselves."

Early next morning Chow Phiwan took his waterpot and walked out into the woods. He came to a clearing where he saw a pond. *This must be the Mohomahang water,* he thought and began filling his pot.

Chow Kem went out and looked around him. Dew drops glistened like shimmering jewels upon every leaf and blade of grass in the forest. He wiped the dew drops from the leaves of the plants and the trees with the towel and squeezed the water into the pot. Working gently and diligently in this manner he was able to fill half his waterpot with dew.

Having completed the task given to them, the two boys placed their waterpots before their teacher and waited for his verdict.

"You both belong to the same kingdom and have been taught the same lessons by me," the teacher said. "How did you get the water I asked for?" he asked the prince.

"There is this big pond which I discovered in the jungle, which I think is the Mohomahang pond. That's where I got the water from," Chow Phiwan answered.

The teacher turned to Chow Kem. "What about you?"

"When I woke up at dawn, the only water I saw around me was the morning dew. I used the towel to collect the dew and squeezed it into the pot," Chow Kem said.

The teacher smiled. "Mohomahang water is indeed dew because it is found early in the morning. You have passed the test. I have taught you all that I know. My blessings are with you." The two boys packed their belongings and took leave of their teacher. They went to the city and purchased two horses to take them back to Aphipataka. They stopped at Visodha and decided to camp on the banks of the river for the night.

Now, in the kingdom of Visodha lived a princess who was famed for her beauty as well as her intelligence. She was named Mokmo, after the lotus. When Chow Soling the Sun God woke up from his slumber each morning, the first thing he saw was the face of the beautiful princess Mokmo. She would always be there, standing by the banks of the river waiting to welcome him with a garland of sweet smelling flowers, which her maid had strung the night before.

When Chow Phiwan went to wash his face that morning, he saw Mokmo on the opposite bank. She had a garland of flowers in her hand and was bathed in golden sunlight. The prince

She would always be there, standing by the banks of the river waiting to welcome him with a garland of sweet smelling flowers.

immediately fell in love with her and told his friend to find out who she was. They both crossed over to the other bank and approached the princess.

"What is your name?" Chow Kem asked politely.

She looked at them and without uttering a single word plucked out a lotus from the garland. She placed the lotus to her heart and let it fall to the ground. Stepping on it she walked away without a backward glance. The prince was puzzled. "Why did she do that? Is she dumb?"

"Certainly not!" Chow Kem replied. "I think she's testing us. Anyway, from her actions it is evident that her name is Mokmo." The prince could only marvel at his friend's keen sense of observation and intelligence. A little distance away they came to a hut where they saw an old woman stringing flowers and making garlands, much like the one Mokmo had been holding. They stopped to enquire.

"Are you making these garlands for Mokmo?" Chow Kem asked. The old woman was taken aback. "How did you know?" She asked.

"Never mind that," Chow Kem replied and sat down next to her. "Allow me to string this garland for you." He took the garland from her and strung it in a different style. The old woman was glad to get help for she was quite fed up of doing the same work every day. When she handed the garland to the princess the next morning, the princess took one look at it and commented, "This does not look like your work. Who strung it for you?"

"I did," lied the maid, not wanting to upset the princess. When the old maid went home she saw the two boys waiting for her. They talked and joked with her and she let them string the garland for her while she made them some tea. The next morning when the princess saw the garland she said, "I am certain this is not your work. Tell me the truth. Who has been making the garlands for you?"

Knowing she was cornered, the old maid confessed, "There are two boys who insist on making the garlands. One of them is a prince and the other one is a minister's son."

Mokmo paced up and down the hallway. "Get me soot from the kitchen" she ordered.

The maid hurried to the kitchen and scraped all the soot off the bottom of the pots. She took it to the princess in a bowl. The princess scooped a handful of soot from the bowl and smeared it over the maid's face. She then pressed her sooty palm on the maid's back and sent her off with a push. The old maid ran home sobbing and told the boys what had happened.

"It's all because of you that the princess is annoyed with me," she cried. "If you hadn't tried to meddle with my work, none of this would have happened. Now look what she's done to my face and back."

Chow Kem looked at her and said, "Don't worry, the princess is not angry with you. She's just conveying a message."

"What do you mean?" Chow Phiwan was puzzled. "She has blackened the old woman's face and you say it's a message she's sending us. Have you gone mad?"

"No! I've not gone mad and neither has the old woman been punished," Chow Kem replied calmly. "The princess says she will meet us after five days on a dark moonless night. You will go and meet her that night."

Just as Chow Kem had predicted, the fifth night was a dark moonless night. Following the directions given by the old maid, Chow Phiwan entered the chamber of the princess. She showed no surprise as though she had been expecting him.

"Was it you who found out my name that day?" she asked. Chow Phiwan may not have been as clever as his friend but he was no liar either. "No, it wasn't me. It was my friend," He replied truthfully.

His friend appears to be very intelligent, the princess thought. They spoke for a while and when it was time for him to leave, she gave him a packet. "Here is some cake for your friend but be careful not to eat it yourself. Come back tomorrow."

Chow Kem took the packet from his friend and asked, "What

exactly did she say to you?"

"She told me not eat the cake but to give it to you and invited me tomorrow night," Chow Phiwan replied. Chow Kem took the cake and fed it to the old maid's dog. Moments later the dog was dead. Chow Phiwan was shocked.

"It could have been you," he exclaimed. "Why would she want you dead?"

"Perhaps this is another test of hers. However, she is a dangerous person and must be stopped," Chow Kem said. "Let me think of something."

The following day, Chow Kem handed the prince a packet of crimson dye. "When you visit the princess, keep her engrossed in stories and fan her to sleep. After she falls asleep, paint a spear on her right thigh and bring her jewellery to me without her knowing it."

"She will have me killed," Chow Phiwan protested.

"No! She won't!" Chow Kem said. "Just do as I say." In the end he convinced the prince to go according to his plan. The princess opened the door and welcomed Chow Phiwan into her chamber.

"Did your friend eat the cake?" she asked sweetly. "Quick! Tell me all. I am impatient to hear it."

Chow Phiwan tried to sound as convincing as possible. "I wonder what was in that cake because the moment he ate it, he fell into a swoon and has not woken up since."

The princess gave a mysterious smile and began removing her jewellery, which she placed on a silk handkerchief on her dressing table. Chow Phiwan told her stories and fanned her till she grew drowsy and fell into a deep slumber. Taking out the crimson dye from his pocket, he painted a spear on her right thigh. He then quietly went to the dressing table and knotted the silk handkerchief with the jewels inside before slipping out into the darkness. Chow Kem was waiting for him. The next morning they discussed their plan for the day.

"Sit on the main crossing and hawk this jewellery, but don't sell it cheap," Chow Kem advised. By now, Chow Phiwan trusted his friend's judgement and did not question him. He went to the busiest crossing and began shouting, "Jewellery for sale! Come and buy these lovely precious gems!" Chow Kem disguised himself as a hermit and sat down under a pipal tree holding a spear in his hand.

Meanwhile the princess had discovered the theft of her jewels and alerted her guards. In no time Chow Phiwan was caught with the stolen property and led away in chains.

"You are under arrest for the theft of the princess's jewels," he was told.

"No! These jewels belong to the hermit sitting under that tree," Chow Phiwan protested. "He asked me to sell them for him. Go, ask him if you don't believe me!" He led them to Chow Kem.

The guards approached the hermit and demanded, "Where did you get these jewels from, thief?"

"I did not steal it," Chow Kem spoke confidently. "Your princess gave them to me. That Puhsu you call a princess danced in front of me all night. I had to spear her on the thigh to chase her off."

By now a large crowd had gathered around the tree. They were shocked at what the hermit had to say about their princess. "Let's go and report this to the king," one of the men said. "We must find out the truth."

They all proceeded to the palace. The king's expression was grim. "You will be put to death if your accusations turn out to be false," he said to Chow Kem.

The princess appeared before the court and was asked to lift her dress. When she did, the crowd gasped, "Look! The mark of the spear! She is a Puhsu! The hermit was right!"

The poor princess looked surprised and confused. *Where did this mark come from? It must be the work of the prince!* She looked accusingly at him.

The king was on the horns of a dilemma. He loved his daughter and did not want to punish her, but he had to satisfy the crowd by projecting himself a just ruler. The assembled crowd demanded that the princess be banished into the forest. "She is a Puhsu and deserves to live among the wild beasts."

The king was powerless and had to bow down to the wishes of the people. He banished his only daughter to the forest to live among the wild animals. The people were satisfied with the verdict and praised the king. Chow Phiwan and Chow Kem were allowed to leave without being questioned about the jewels in their possession. They rode into the forest and came to a little hut, which had been built to accommodate the banished princess. Upon seeing them, Mokmo burst into tears. "What do you want now?" she asked. She was no more the ruthless princess but a very vulnerable girl.

"We have come to return your jewellery," Chow Phiwan said. "We are on our way home so if you like you may accompany us." Mokmo was only too pleased to get out of the forest. She went to Aphipataka with the two young men and upon their arrival was married off to Chow Phiwan, with the blessings of Chow Kem.

32

Ai Mao, Ngee Hunangyow and Sam Songpha

A very long time ago there lived a poor farmer and his wife who had three sons named Ai Mao, Ngee Hunangyow and Sam Songpha. The farmer and his wife were very hard working and did all they could to provide a comfortable life for their sons, hoping that some day their sons would strike it rich. Much to their disappointment, the three brothers turned out to be good for nothing. All they did was laze around and dream of the good things in life without actually working towards it.

The old couple could not bear to see their sons wasting their lives. "If you carry on like this no girl will ever marry any of you," the mother said. That set them thinking.

"Mother, I will go out into the world and seek my fortune," the eldest son Ai Mao said.

"All right son, I shall tell your father to give you his axe," the mother said. "It will bring you luck."

Ai Mao took the axe and bid his parents and two brothers goodbye. He walked and walked till he came to spot from where he could see a tall banyan tree atop a hill.

I shall cut down the tree and make a fortune selling all that wood, he thought while climbing up the hill. Ai Mao swung his axe and began hacking at the tree with all his might. He worked non-stop for seven days and seven nights until at last the tree gave way. It came down with a mighty crash, waking up the giant from whose ear it grew.

The giant sat up with a start and grabbed Ai Mao in a flash. He narrowed his eyes to have a better look at his captive, whom he held in his hands. "So!" he roared. "It was you that was annoying me all these days and nights with your constant knocking. I could barely sleep."

Ai Mao quivered in fright. He had never met a giant before and here he was in the grip of a giant and an angry one at that too.

"I'll have to eat you for disturbing my sleep," the giant said, opening his cavernous mouth and exposing a row of yellow teeth the size of boulders.

"Wait! Wait!" Ai Mao yelled frantically. "I'm too tiny to satisfy your hunger. You may eat my brothers who are fatter than me. They're not far from here." The giant blinked his eyes a couple of times as he mulled over the suggestion. "Brothers you say? That sounds good, but where do I find them?"

"I'll show you the way, but you must help me carry this tree," Ai Mao said. The giant put him down and Ai Mao quickly ran towards the branches of the tree. "I'll carry the tree from this end and you can lift it from the other end."

Ai Mao climbed up a branch and shouted, "Come on, lift the tree from your end and let's carry it." The foolish giant lifted the tree over his shoulders and carried it for miles with Ai Mao pointing out the way. When Ai Mao neared his home he shouted out, "Stop! Let's put the tree down here. We've reached our destination." The giant gladly put the tree down and Ai Mao jumped to the ground. The giant was very tired and he wondered how it was that the little man seemed unaffected by it all.

He must be very strong. Much stronger than me despite his size, the giant thought. *I'd better be nice to him.*

"I have an aunt who lives inside a stone deep down under the ocean," the giant confided. "My aunt possesses a magic ring that can give you anything you wish for."

"How do I get that ring, if I may ask you?" Ai Mao asked.

The giant sighed. "Only I can swim that deep and fetch the

ring. No one else knows which part of the ocean it lies in."

Ai Mao desperately wanted the ring. He also realized that the giant was foolish enough to get it for him. "Well, I want that ring," he said in a commanding voice. "Get it for me or my brothers will make you get it."

"Don't worry, I'll go there at once," the giant said.

"How do I know if you are speaking the truth?" Ai Mao asked. "You'll have to give me a gaurantee."

The giant pulled out a stand of hair from his golden locks and handed it to Ai Mao. "If I fail to come, you just have to split the hair apart and I shall be with you in an instant," he said before leaving.

Three days had gone by and there was no sign of the giant. Ai Mao was getting impatient. He took out the giant's hair and carefully split it apart. The pain was too much for the giant to bear. He had gone off to sleep thinking Ai Mao would not be in such a hurry but he was wrong. Quick as a flash, he dived into the ocean and stole the magic ring from his old aunt. A few leaps and bounds later he reached Ai Mao.

The giant handed him the magic ring, which turned out so large that Ai Mao could easily pass through it. "What am I supposed to do with it?" Ai Mao asked the giant.

"Cover the ring with a piece of white muslin and at the stroke of midnight, make your wish," the giant said. "Now that you have got what you wanted, can I go back to sleep?"

Ai Mao placed the ring on the ground and covered it with a piece of white muslin. "Spirit of the ring, turn this humble hut into a mansion," he said at the stroke of midnight. There was a whoosh and the next instant a magnificient stone mansion stood before him in place of his old home. Over the next few days Ai Mao made more wishes and they were all fulfilled. He was now the richest and most repected person in the village. His parents were very proud of his achievements and his brothers longed to be as lucky but they were too lazy to venture out.

One day the farmer called his second son Ngee Hunangyow

aside and spoke to him. "Son, your brother has made his fortune. Are you going to spend the rest of your life living in his shadow or will you go out and seek your fortune like him?" Ngee Hunangyow felt ashamed and decided to leave at once. His father gave him a knife and wished him success.

Ngee Hunangyow walked for days through meadows and hills. He took a narrow path, which was so overgrown that while cutting his way through the bushes, his nose got entangled in a creeper. When he tried to pull the creeper off he found to his horror that his nose had grown so long it touched his knees. Frightened out of his wits, he tried to free himself, but his nose got in the way. It got entangled in the bushes and slowed him down by causing him to trip and fall. Taking a deep breath he accidently sniffed another creeper that was stuck to his nose. No sooner had he done it than his nose was sucked all the way in till only his nostrils remained. He touched his face and cried out in alarm when he found his nose missing. Frantically he tore at every creeper and sniffed at them until he found the creeper that made his nose grow long again. Then taking the creeper that made his nose disappear, he sniffed them both alternately until his nose was back to its original length. He took both creepers and kept them carefully in his pocket before proceeding further.

Ngee Hunangyow continued walking till he came to a kingdom where the princess was said to be so stunningly beautiful that her presence itself could illuminate seven rooms. The king held an annual assembly in which all suitors for the hand of the princess were shown a bowl and asked to fill it to the brim with gold. The amount of gold had to be so precise that a little less or a little more would disqualify the competitor and land him in prison. He was then bound to serve a five-year sentence whereby his duty would be to fetch and pour water over the princess while she bathed.

Of the five men who were serving out their sentence, three happened to be from the same kingdom as Ngee Hunangyow. One of them was the prince. They were tired of fetching and pouring water over the princess everyday and wanted to go home but they could not find a way out. Ngee Hunangyow introduced himself and said, "Don't worry, I have a solution to your problem." He gave the first creeper to the prince and told him to put it in his waterpot.

Sam Songpha strapped the basket to his back and went merrily on his way.

When the prince poured the water over the princess, her nose grew and grew until it resembled a fat worm. Her maids jumped out of the bath and ran away screaming in fright at the sight of the princess who now looked like a hedious monster. The king and queen came running and fainted when they saw their beautiful daughter in such a terrible state.

After the king had recovered he made an important announcement. "Whosoever cures the princess shall marry her and get half my kingdom as reward."

That was just what Ngee Hunangyow was waiting for. He wasted no time in stepping forward to save the princess. "I have the cure. Put a screen around the princess and allow me to begin my treatment." A screen was put around the bath and the princess waited anxiously, trying to hide her ugly face from view.

Ngee Hunangyow took two waterpots and put the creeper that shortened the nose in one pot and the creeper that elongated the nose in the second pot. He took the first pot and poured some water over the princess. Her long nose wriggled and with a sudden jerk vanished out of sight, leaving two holes where her nose should have been. Ngee Hunangyow quickly took the second pot and poured water over the princess. This time her nose grew till her chin. Alternating between the two pots, Ngee Hunangyow was able to get the nose of the princess to its original size. The princess shrieked with happiness when she saw her reflection in the mirror. Her beauty now restored to its former glory, the princess once again lit up seven rooms with her presence.

The king and queen were extremely grateful. "We give you our daughter as promised and half the kingdom too," the king said.

"I am only a poor farmer's son, your majesty," replied Ngee Hunangyow. "The princess would be far happier if she married the prince." The princess was only too willing to marry the prince instead of Ngee Hunangyow, for though he had cured her, he did not appeal to her. The grateful prince built him a grand palace and gave his own sister in marriage to Ngee Hunangyow.

Seeing that his two elder brothers had been so successful in their quest, the youngest son Sam Songpha grew restless. "I too want to go out into the world and seek my fortune," he told his parents.

His parents gave him their blessings and a huge cane basket. "Take this basket and go seek your fortune," his mother said. "It is the only thing we have. The rest belong to your brothers."

Sam Songpha strapped the basket to his back and went merrily on his way. Every now and then he bent down to pick up bits and pieces of clay, wood, pebbles etc; and threw them into his basket. "Who knows? I might need it in the future," he would say to himself as he picked up a piece of something he had no idea about. By and by his basket grew so heavy with all the odds and ends thrown in, that he had trouble balancing himself.

Sam Songpha somehow managed to reach a little town where he stopped to rest under the shade of a tree. People stopped by wondering if he had something to sell. "What do you have in the basket?" a woman asked him.

"It's full of my belongings," Sam Songpha proudly replied. Not far from where he sat, he could see people crowding over something. Sam Songpha went to investigate. Everyone seemed to be bending down to look into a pit.

"What's inside the pit?" he asked the man standing next to him.

"The king is searching for a brave and fearless man to be his army commander. Whoever jumps into the pit will be made the commander," the man told him.

"Is it very deep?" Sam Songpha asked.

"It is not only deep but the bottom is lined with sharp spikes," the man replied. "Only a fool would dare jump in."

"Let me see it," Sam Songpha said and pushed his way through the crowd to the front. He bent down to have a look. The pit was very deep and like the man had said, was lined with rows and rows of sharp steel spikes. The spikes glinted as they caught the rays of the sun. Indeed, only a reckless fool would dare jump in. Instead of becoming the army commander he would surely go to paradise. Sam Songpha had no wish to go to paradise so early. He was yet to find his fortune. Shuddering at the thought of falling in, he straightened himself, but the heavy basket made him lose his balance and sent him somersaulting into the pit.

"Aaaaah!" his voice echoed as he hit the bottom. The crowd bent down to look at the poor man who had fallen in, expecting to find him speared to death. Nothing of that sort happened. Sam Songpha opened his eyes to find himself sitting on a soft bed of cotton camouflaged with brown earth. The sharp steel spears were nothing but spears fashioned out of silver paper. It was just a trick to see if there was anyone brave enough to jump into the pit.

Sam Songpha was hauled out of the pit, taken to the barber where he was given a proper shave and bathed in warm scented water. He was made the commander of the king's army and although his basket was damaged in the fall, he kept it as a reminder of his old days.

The farmer and his wife were at last satisfied with the way all their three sons had managed to find their fortunes.

33

Along Cham Kam

A long time ago there lived a king who proudly considered himself as being the source of all good luck. If anything happened around him that was good, he would say, "It's all due to my luck." One day the king and his minister Chow Amat went out for a picnic in the countryside. After a very enjoyable day, they decided to return to the palace.

"If not for me and my luck we surely would not have had such a good time," the king said as usual. Fed up of the king's boastfulness, Chow Amat replied, "It's neither your luck nor my luck that we had a nice day, your majesty. It is all due to our combined luck."

Not used to being corrected the king gave him a dirty glare. "Nonsense! It's only because of me that everything good happens." Chow Amat was not one to give up so easily and so the two kept on arguing till they decided to go their separate ways to see who was luckier.

Chow Amat went deep into the jungle and came upon a strange sight. Sobbing under a tree was the demon Nang Phai with the body of her dead husband across her lap. She had been sitting in the same position without food and water for the past three years and was reduced to skin and bones.

Chow Amat felt sorry for Nang Phai. "Leave him for he is dead and will not come back to life," he said to her. "We all have to die some day." Chow Amat then went on to explain to her the universal truth of life and death. No one had spoken to Nang Phai

The Chokis gladly brought the three articles and handed them over to the king.

ever since the death of her husband and she was overcome with gratitude.

"You have made me realize how foolish I have been to hope that he would come back to life," she said. "I am happy and grateful that you have made me see reason. What shall I give you? Alas, I have nothing but I will let you into a secret! Go ahead until you come to a place where you will see two ponds side by side. Bathing in one pond will turn you into a monkey and bathing in the other one will turn you into a handsome man." Nang Phai gave him two pots, and then went on to cremate her dead husband's body.

Chow Amat followed Nang Phai's directions and reached the spot she had described. He filled one pot with water from the pond *that turned man into monkey* and the second pot with water from the pond *that made people more beautiful.* Carrying the pots he went back to look for the king.

The king had gone northwards and he had covered quite a distance when he saw two Chokis grappling with one another. They were so engrossed in their fight that they did not notice the king watching them. Quite used to settling disputes, the king went forward and commanded them to stop. "Why are you fighting?" he asked.

"We are trying to divide our father's property and my brother always gets more than me," one of the Chokis said.

The other one immediately flew at his throat, "That's a lie!" he shrieked. "He's the one who always takes more."

"What are the two of you fighting over?" the king asked. The Chokis told him that their father had left them a gong, a fan and a walking stick and ever since then the two of them had not been able to divide the property equally.

"Why don't you let me divide it for you? Bring me your father's property and I will give you both an equal share." The king said. The Chokis gladly brought the three articles and handed them over to the king. The king gave the gong to one brother and the fan to the other one.

"I shall keep the walking stick as my fee," he said. "Now you have nothing to complain about because both of you have been given an equal share of your father's property."

The Chokis thanked him profusely for putting an end to their squabble and flew happily away. Satisfied with the turn of events, the king tapped the ground with his new stick. Lo and behold! A gold coin appeared out of thin air from under the stick. The king picked up the coin and inspected it from all angles to see if it was real. "It is gold!" he muttered and tapped the ground with the stick once more. The same thing happened. Everytime the stick touched the ground, a gold coin appeared from beneath it as if by magic.

Tucking the stick under his arm, the king walked on, trying to find his way back home, but he only managed to wander further and further away from his kingdom. Many days later he found himself in another country where he had no trouble finding a good place to stay, for he had his magic walking stick. After he had bathed and eaten a lavish meal, the king went out for a stroll in the garden near the royal palace. There he saw a long line of men in royal attire carrying water from a well and moving towards the palace grounds. There were ninety-nine of them in total.

The king walked up to them and said, "From your appearance it seems to me that you are of royal blood. Why and for whom are you carrying water from this well?"

"Some of us are kings and some of us are princes and nobles. We came here hoping to win the hand of the beautiful princess but we lost the bet and now we are her slaves. Her father, the emperor of this land wants a thousand cartloads of gold in exchange for his daughter. Even a little less means a lifetime of having to fetch water from this well for the princess's bath."

I must somehow save them from this cruel fate, the king pondered as he took out his stick and tapped it on the ground. Gold tumbled out with every little tap. He worked tirelessly day and night, filling up the carts he had ordered from the palace, until only three carts remained to be filled. So tired was he that he dozed off while still at work. As he slept, one of the emperor's guards came and took away his walking stick and gave it to the emperor. They arrested him and made him fetch water along with the ninety-nine others.

Meanwhile, Chow Amat had grown tired of waiting for the king to return. He was worried something might have happened to the king and followed the tracks that led him straight to the same house where the king had stayed. While walking in the garden, Chow Amat saw the long line of men carrying water from the well. As he went closer he saw the king among them.

"What are you doing here, your majesty?" he asked. The king was happy to see him and told him all that had happened. "Meet me later," Chow Amat said. "I shall be waiting for you right here."

When the king came at the appointed time, Chow Amat handed him the pot that contained the water *which turned man into monkey*. "Take this and pour it over the princess."

When the king poured the water over the princess, she turned into a monkey. She shrieked and jumped about, sending all her maids, the kings and guards running helter skelter. There was utter confusion as the monkey climbed onto the rooftop and refused to come down from her perch. The servants failed in their attempts to catch her. The emperor was in acute distress. "Get someone to cure my daughter," he commanded his men.

Messengers were sent far and wide, announcing a handsome reward to anyone who could restore the princess back to normal. Chow Amat met one of the messengers and asked, "What does the emperor want?"

"He's looking for someone to cure the princess," the man replied. "Can you do it?"

"I may be able to, but if I fail, the emperor will make me one of his slaves so I dare not even try," Chow Amat said. The messenger reported the conversation to the emperor. The emperor immediately sent for Chow Amat.

"I am willing to give you anything you want if you can cure my daughter," he said.

"I want the walking stick that rightfully belongs to my king and I also want all the kings, princes and nobles released at once if I succeed," Chow Amat replied.

The emperor did not hesitate, "Agreed! You will get the walking stick and I shall have all of them released as soon as my daughter is restored to her normal self."

The monkey was finally caught and brought down. Chow

Amat poured the water which *makes people even more beautiful than they are* over the monkey. Sure enough the princess was restored to her original form. Only this time she was lovelier than before.

The emperor was so pleased that he made a grand announcement. "I hand over my beautiful daughter to Chow Amat and also a part of my kingdom." He also returned the walking stick and freed all the kings, princes and nobles who were held captive.

Chow Amat was engaged to the princess but he had no love for her and asked the emperor's permission to go back to his country. The emperor refused to allow him, for he had a grand wedding planned ahead. Chow Amat pleaded, saying he could only get married in his own country with his parents' blessings. The emperor at last agreed to let him go.

Chow Amat, the princess and the king started off on their journey. When they reached their own kingdom, Chow Amat asked the king to accept the princess as his bride. "I am just a minister and the princess is fit to be a queen," he said. The princess was married off to the king and when the excitement was over, Chow Amat took the king aside and said, "Never again say it is your luck. Remember, it is the combined luck of everyone that makes things work out for the better." The king for once had to agree wholeheartedly that his minister was right.

Choki: Flying spirits that can cure ailments; Along: Royalty; Cham: Test; Kam: Luck; Amat: Minister

34

Kemisanta & Chow Naracheta

Long, long ago, there lived the son of a nobleman whose name was Naracheta. He was young, brave, handsome and much admired. Chow Sekay, the overlord of paradise noticed the admirable qualities of Naracheta and wanted him as a son-in-law. He drew a portrait of his beautiful daughter Kemisanta and flew down to earth with it. Disguising himself as an old man he went up to Naracheta and gifted him the picture bound in gold cloth.

When Naracheta gazed upon Kemisanta's portrait, he fell hopelessly in love with the girl and wondered who she was. He showed the picture to his friend and the two of them went high and low looking for the old man who had given him the portrait, but they could find no trace of him. Naracheta became depressed and slowly his health deteriorated. He hardly ate or slept and his worried parents reluctantly allowed him to go in search of the mysterious girl. His friend accompanied him in his quest. They boarded a ship that sailed far out into sea where strong winds and giant waves tossed the hapless ship about like a toy and dashed it against a rocky shore. Everyone on board including Narcheta's friend died in the shipwreck except for Naracheta. He watched terrified as Phephais appeared out of the woods and devoured the dead. Seeing that he was conscious, a Phephai lifted him and carried him deep into the woods to Maung Phai. The Phephai princess fell in love with him and ordered that no one should harm him. She sang and danced for him and proposed marriage to him. Naracheta told her that he could not marry her because his heart belonged to someone else. The heartbroken Phephai princess let him go for she truly loved him, although she had the power to keep him prisoner.

Naracheta walked a great distance until he came to a cave with a huge door that was guarded by a tiger on one side and a goat on the other. There was meat lying next to the goat and a bundle of grass next to the tiger. Naracheta took the meat and placed it in front of the tiger. He took the grass and placed it in front of the goat. As soon as the animals took the food that was offered to them, the door slid open on its own. Naracheta entered the cave and looked around. He found a girl lying asleep next to a golden stick. When he picked up the stick the girl woke up.

"Who are you?" Naracheta asked the girl.

"I am a princess from a far off land. Phai Loam kidnapped me and has kept me imprisoned in this dark cave for a long time," she said. "Please help me escape."

"We will have to find a way to kill him otherwise he would follow us even if we tried to escape," Naracheta said. "Does he have any weakness?"

"It won't be easy killing him for he wears an amulet around his neck. It protects him from all harm," the princess replied.

Naracheta felt very sorry for the princess. "Do as I tell you and we will get out of this cave," he said, and was about to tell her his plans when he heard a loud whoosh.

"It's him. Go and hide," the frightened girl whispered and laying the stick next to her body she went off to sleep. Phai Loam entered the cave and sniffed about suspiciously. He lifted the stick and the princess woke up.

"I can smell a man inside this cave," he told her. "Has anyone been here while I was away?"

"Who will dare come in?" the princess replied. "You forget I am a human too, so maybe it is me that you smell."

How is it that I never smelled something like this before? It's a strange kind of man smell, Phai Loam wondered, still not convinced. The princess was afraid he would discover Naracheta so she quickly stood in front of Phai Loam and said, "I am all grown up now and ready to be someone's wife. Let us get married, but first you will have to go and inform your relatives. Invite them to our wedding feast."

Phai Loam looked at the girl before him. She was very beautiful and he would be the envy of all the Phephais if she became his wife. He rushed off to inform his relatives who lived on the other side of the world. As soon as he left, Naracheta came out of his hiding place and told the princess what she had to do. When they heard Phai Loam approaching, Naracheta went back to his hiding place and the princess put the stick next to her and lay down to sleep.

Phai Loam was in a happy mood. He picked up the stick and when the princess woke up from her sleep, he told her, "I have informed all my relatives and they will arrive here tomorrow for the wedding."

"You must be tired after the long journey," the princess said. "Go to sleep so that you wake up fresh for our wedding tomorrow." Phai Loam was indeed very tired and as soon as his head touched the ground he was snoring away. The princess removed the amulet from around Phai Loam's neck and passed it on to Naracheta, who threw it away. He then took Phai Loam's axe and killed him.

The princess opened a box and took out some pills. "These pills will make it possible for us to live without food and water for three months at a time," she said. "We may need it for our journey."

Kemisanta at once went back to Maungphe and returned with an army of female warriors.

The two of them hurried out of the cave and travelled for many weeks and months till they reached the home of the princess. Naracheta showed her the picture of the girl he was searching for. The princess looked at the picture and exclaimed, "That's my cousin Kemisanta!"

Naracheta's heart was filled with happiness. At long last he was close to finding the girl of his dreams and he already found out her name. He begged the princess to introduce him to her cousin.

"She does not live here," the princess told him. "Her home is in Maungphe, but I will try and send a message for her to come here."

When Kemisanta received the message from her cousin, she went to her father and said, "I am curious to go down to earth and see who this Naracheta is. My cousin tells me that he has been searching for me." Chow Sekay smiled to himself. His plan was working.

Kemisanta flew down to earth on her gleaming chariot and when she was introduced to Naracheta she asked him, "How did you come to know of me?"

Naracheta took out the picture he always carried with him and showed it to her. "An old man gave it to me and I have never seen him again, but I've been searching for you ever since."

Kemisanta looked at her picture and immediately recognized her father's handiwork. She knew her father must have found Naracheta highly eligible or he would not have taken the trouble to go through with this sort of plan. Kemisanta herself felt attracted to the brave and handsome Naracheta and when he proposed to her, she willingly accepted.

"I must first inform my father," Kemisanta said. "I shall not be gone for long." She boarded her chariot and disappeared into the skies, leaving Naracheta waiting for her.

Naracheta could not believe his good fortune at having met the beautiful Kemisanta of his dreams. He thought of her day and night as he waited for her to return. In the meantime, the relatives of Phai Loam had come to the cave for the wedding feast and when they found him dead, they searched high and low for the person responsible for his death. With the help of their magic and keen sense of smell, the Phephais were able to trace Naracheta.

"You are responsible for the death of our brother," the Phephais shrieked and grabbed him. They took him to Maung Phai and threw him into a deep well from which no man could escape.

When Kemisanta returned, her cousin informed her of Naracheta's abduction by a horde of fierce Phephais. Kemisanta at once went back to Maungphe and returned with an army of female warriors. She led her army against the Phephais and a fierce battle was fought. The Phephais were no match for the female warriors from Maungphe and before long admitted defeat. Naracheta was rescued from the well and reunited with Kemisanta.

Maung Phai: Land of the demons; Maungphe: Paradise; Phai Loam: **Wind** demon

35

Luk Khoi the Son-in-law

Yaekok, a very loving and dutiful daughter lived with her old parents high up in the mountains far away from civilization. Her parents were worried that they would not be able to find a groom for their daughter because of their inability to go anywhere. There were no visitors and it had been many years since they had travelled to the nearest village, which was on the other side of the mountain.

"What will happen to Yaekok after we are gone?' the old woman lamented. The old man was an optimist. "With the Lord's blessing's she will be fine. There's no point in worrying."

Yaekok on her part had no such worries. She was happy playing the good and dutiful daughter and basked in the affection of her parents. Then one fine day all that changed with the sudden arrival of a young man who had lost his way and had nowhere to stay.

"You can stay with us," the old woman said. "What is your name?"

"My name is Luk Khoi," replied the young man, smiling broadly at Yaekok. The old couple welcomed him into their home and secretly hoped that he would marry their daughter. They need not have worried, for the young man soon had Yaekok under his spell and the two of them became inseperable.

Yaekok's parents were happy with the way things had turned out. Their daughter would now be taken care of after they were gone. Yaekok considered herself very lucky to have found such a

"At last! My wife has spoken twice," Luk Khoi remarked. He removed the hai khow from the fire with the help of the tongs and served the rice and eggs for his wife and himself.

loving husband without having to move out of her own home. She could not have asked for more. Both husband and wife shared the workload and in the evenings they would all sit by the fire. Luk Khoi would tell them stories about his village and the world that was alien to Yaekok. She would listen enthralled and never tire of hearing the same story a hundred times over. Luk Khoi however soon tired of life in the mountains and longed to return to the valley.

"Let us go to my village and start a new life together," Luk Khoi told his wife one day.

"And what about my parents?" Yaekok asked him. "Who will cook their food and look after them if we left?"

Luk Khoi tried to convince his wife to leave but she was not willing to listen. When he tried to explain his point of view, she sulked and refused to answer him. Luk Khoi could have left on his own but he loved his wife dearly and wanted to take her along. One day while sitting on the banks of the river, he had a brilliant idea. If he went downstream he would certainly come across some village and it would be easy to find his way home from there.

For the next few days Luk Khoi went about putting his plan into action. He felled a sturdy tree and worked from morning to night carving out a boat.

"What are you making?" Yaekok asked him.

"It's a boat," he explained. "We can go and fetch a lot of firewood if we have a boat." Yaekok thought her husband was very clever. Her parents too thought the same.

There was a lot of excitement the day the boat was ready. "We shall leave tomorrow morning," Luk Khoi announced. "Get the hai khow, some rice and eggs for we shall be gone the whole day and return only by nightfall." Yaekok was excited as well as a little apprehensive about travelling on a boat.

"What a clever son-in-law we have," the old woman said to her husband. "We are lucky to have found him."

Luk Khoi and Yaekok woke up very early the next day and after Yaekok had prepared the day's meal for her parents, the two of them set out on their journey. They passed through forests abundant in firewood, but Luk Khoi did not stop.

"Are we not going too far away?" Yaekok asked anxiously. "Why don't we stop to collect firewood?"

"Wait a bit," Luk Khoi told her. "We still have to go a little further." The boat took them out of the forests and through fields of ripe corn. Yaekok could see huts along the way and people working in the fields.

"There are no forests here," Yaekok was beginning to feel uneasy. "Let's go back the way we came." Luk Khoi pretended not to hear her. He rowed faster and faster until they came to a village that looked familiar to him. Stopping the boat, Luk Khoi hopped out of the boat and began unloading the provisions.

"Let's cook some food. I'm hungry," he said, and lit a fire on the bank. Yaekok stood near the boat and said, "I want to go home. I'm not hungry."

Taking no notice of her, Luk Khoi took out an egg and said, "I am going to have roasted eggs." He took a stick and tried to skewer the egg.

"Idiot!" Yaekok shouted at him. "That's not the way to cook an egg. You have to boil it."

"At last! My wife has spoken once," Luk Khoi smiled at her. He took the eggs and put them to boil while his wife watched sullenly.

"Now let's cook some rice," Luk Khoi announced. He put the rice in the hai khow and tucked the tongs into his waistband. When the rice was cooked he circled the fire muttering loudly, "Where did I keep my tongs? I saw it just a while ago."

"Fool!" his wife snapped. "It's tucked into your waistband or have you gone blind?"

"At last! My wife has spoken twice," Luk Khoi remarked. He removed the hai khow from the fire with the help of the tongs and served the rice and eggs for his wife and himself. They both ate in silence. The sun had set and it was growing chilly. Luk Khoi spread out the bedding and pitched up the mosquito net over it making it look like a nice and cosy tent. He walked around the net in circles prompting his wife to ask, "What are you looking for?"

"I'm looking for a way to get in," Luk Khoi answered.

"Foolish man! This is how you do it," Yaekok snapped, as she lifted the net and crawled in.

"At last! My wife has spoken thrice," Luk Khoi sighed happily and followed her in. And so it goes without saying that the two of them lived happily ever after.

Luk Khoi: Son-in-law; Hai khow: Rice steamer

36

The Good Wife

Two very good friends Nok and Keli were married to women of very different temperament. Nok was married to a sweet natured girl and they lived a quiet and peaceful life. Keli on the other hand was married to a shrew, who nagged him all the while and treated him like a slave.

"What have you been doing all day?" she would ask her husband after she had come back from visiting the neighbour's house. "Have you locked the chicken in? What about the cows? Have you milked them?" Woe betide him if he had forgotten all these tasks, or if he had forgotten to bring in the firewood, or fill the waterpots or have the fire burning.

The neighbours felt sorry for poor Keli, though they also thought that he was not man enough to stand up to his bully of a wife. She dictated what he should do, where he should go and whom he should talk to and so on and so forth. Keli was so used to listening to her, that he stopped thinking for himself. At least there was peace in the house if he agreed to her demands.

Then one day his old friend Nok came visiting. Keli's wife had gone out as usual so he was able to entertain his friend without interferance from her. Nok had a lot to talk about. He told Keli about how lucky he was to have married such a sweet natured and hard working woman and asked Keli about his wife.

"What can I say to you? Everyone in this village knows of my wife's temperament so I cannot lie to you," Keli replied, shamefaced.

Keli's wife went to the forest with her friends to collect plantain leaves.

"Why, what do you mean by that?" Nok was curious to know. Keli hesitantly told his friend about what a difficult person his wife was and how miserable he felt. Nok felt sorry for his friend.

"Maybe I could bring about a change in her attitude," he said.

Keli was taken aback. "How will you be able to do that? She does even let others finish their sentence, so don't even think of trying to teach her. It will be useless, like talking to a stone."

"Just trust me, friend," Nok smiled and patted his friend encouragingly. "You wait and see." When Keli's wife returned home in the evening, she was annoyed that her husband had not done the chores she had told him to, but because Nok was present, she did not say much. However, she made a great deal of noise banging the pots and pans in an attempt to show her displeasure.

Next morning Keli's wife went to the forest with her friends to collect plantain leaves. Nok went to the kitchen and scraped off a good amount of soot from the bottom of the kettle and collected a bagful of chicken feathers. Keeping himself out of sight, he followed the women into the forest. He watched them as they went deeper into the forest to cut the leaves, which were bundled and kept under a banyan tree. The weary women rested for a while before venturing out to collect more leaves. Nok had in the meantime painted his face with soot and glued his body with the chicken feathers. As soon as the women were out of sight he climbed up the banyan tree and lay in wait.

After sometime the women returned and once again they rested under the tree. Nok jumped down from the tree with a growl and caught hold of Keli's wife in a tight embrace. Seeing him, the other women fled in terror, leaving Keli's wife to her fate. The terrified woman screamed and shouted for help but there was no one to come to her aid.

"Help me!" she cried out in panic. "Help! I'm about to be killed."

The more she yelled, the tighter the feathered monster gripped her. "I am Phee Tonehoong. I heard that you ill treat your husband."

"No! No!" she pleaded. "I'll never do it again. Let lightening strike me dead if I lie." The monster did not loosen his grip.

"If you break your promise, I shall come after you in the form of a mouse," the monster hissed. Keli's wife promised to reform. She promised to be a good wife and look after her husband. She promised never to nag him and to do all the housework herself. The monster finally let her go. She went home shaken from the experience, but kept her bargain with Phee Tonehoong a secret from everyone including her husband.

Keli was about to pick up a pile of firewood and carry it up the steps when his wife returned home, her hair and clothes a mess and feathers sticking to her. Before he could ask her what had happened she ran up to him and snatched the firewood from his hands.

"Here, let me take it," she said and carried it up the steps to their kitchen. Keli was surprised. He took the empty waterpot and was going out to fetch the water when his wife stopped him. "No, you don't have to do it. I'll go and fetch the water from now onwards."

Keli was more than surprised at this sudden change in his wife. He silently thanked his dear friend.

Keli's wife kept her promise. She did all the work in the house and did not nag her husband at all. If she ever heard a mouse scurrying about she would quickly reach out for her husband and in her sweetest tone ask, "Shall I fan you?" or "Shall I press your legs?" Keli became the most envied man in the entire village.

Phee Tonehoong: Spirit of the Banyan tree

37

Pona Changsang and the Spirit Judge

Pona Changsang was a wise old man who liked to go for long walks along the river bank not far from his home. In his younger days Pona Changsang was fond of fishing and it was not unusual for him to take a raft and scour the river for a good place to cast his net. He remembered the good old days when he would go on fishing expeditions with friends. If only he could find some youngster who would willingly catch some fish for him so that he could have a feast. Oh, what a feast that would be!

Pona Changsang sat hunched over the bank and peered into the crystal clear water. He could see little fishes darting to and fro among the stones in the bottom. Just then a huge silvery fish swam into view. Pona Changsang felt he could almost touch it, if he waded into the water. He looked longingly at the fish and counted the many ways in which he would cook it, had he caught it.

He started off with the tail end. First of all, he would fry the tail to a crisp and have it with his rice beer. Next, he would salt and smoke the middle portion over burning coals. That might even take an entire evening but the effort would be worth it. If the fish had eggs, which looking by the size of it seemed most probable, he would boil the eggs with herbs and have it for dinner. The last and most delicious part of it, the head, would be soaked in herbs and steamed. Pona Changsang smacked his lips and could almost taste the fish that was still very much alive and swimming. Alas! If he could somehow turn his dreams into reality.

All along, the Great Spirit judge was jotting down Pona

Changsang's evil thoughts. When the weight of his evil intentions became too heavy, the spirit judge revealed himself and caught hold of Pona Changsang. The old man was taken by surprise. He tried to wriggle out of the grasp of the spirit judge, but Pona Changsang was no longer the strong youngster of old. His efforts only caused him to wheeze and pant. He began to understand how a dying fish must feel.

"Where are you taking me?" Pona Changsang asked his grim faced captor. "What crime have I committed?"

"I am taking you to hell, where you will be thrown into a pot of boiling water." The spirit judge replied without any emotion. "I have been observing you and I think you deserve to be punished."

The spirit judge lifted Pona Changsang effortlessly and carried him away to hell. Along the way Pona Changsang saw a

They were flying past a hill when Pona Changsng remarked, "This is the ideal place to build a pagoda. How beautiful it would look."

beautiful green meadow. "Wouldn't it be nice if I were able to build a temple here? It would benefit all of mankind," he pointed out. The spirit judge heard him, but did not reply.

They were flying past a hill when Pona Changsng remarked, "This is the ideal place to build a pagoda. How beautiful it would look." Again the spirit judge heard him, but did not stop.

They were now gliding along a river bank when Pona Changsang remarked, "What a lovely spot to build a rest house for pilgrims."

The spirit judge stopped in his tracks and let go of the old man. His good intentions having outweighed the bad, he had become too hot and heavy for the spirit judge to carry him any further.

"You are free to go because your thoughts have become pure," the spirit judge told Pona Changsang and led him back to his home.

Pona Changsang did not give up eating fish, but he learnt to respect the life of other creatures. He also learnt that thoughts count as much as action, for it is thought that is the seed of all action.

38

Chow Nong Long, Master of the Great Lake

The virtuous monk Chowmone Mangkhom, religiously practiced the most austere penances and was blessed with divine powers. Not far from the village in which the monk lived, was a very huge lake said to be inhabited by the fierce man eating naka named Chow Nong Long, who could transform himself into anything he so desired.

The people living in the surrounding area avoided the lake for fear of encountering Chow Nong Long. Children were not allowed to play in the fields and grown ups hurried home before dusk. Chowmone Mangkhom decided to have a talk with Chow Nong Long and convince him to give up his man-eating tendencies. When he told the villagers of his plan they were appalled.

"Don't go," they pleaded. "Chow Nong Long cannot be reformed by anyone. Your life will be at stake." They did their best to dissuade him from leaving, but Chowmone Mangkhom was made of sterner stuff. He was not afraid of challenges.

He made a raft with help from the villagers and ignoring their pleas, steered himself to the center of the lake, where he began his chanting. At first nothing happened, but as the chanting progressed, there was the sound of a distant rumble from beneath the lake. Chow Naka was slowly waking up from his slumber and he was keen to show his displeasure at having been disturbed while resting. The water began to bubble and boil and huge waves came crashing down upon the raft, tossing it about like a plaything.

The villagers watched helplessly as the fury of Chow Nong Long was being unleashed upon the monk. They saw the monk and his raft disappear under the giant waves only to reappear and disappear again and again everytime the waves bore down on him. When the waves finally subsided and the lake was placid once more, there was no sign of the monk. He seemed to have disappeared without a trace in the middle of the lake.

While the villagers had given up their monk for dead, Chowmone Mangkhom was still very much alive. The waves had thrown him overboard into the murky depths of the world of the

Chow Nong Long stretched himself out of the water to his full height and said, "You will know me!"

nakas. Scaly nakas dragged him to the cave of the mighty Chow Nong Long who was curious to see what the brave monk looked like.

"What is it you want from me?" Chow Nong Long hissed, his eyes cold and glassy. Chowmone Mangkhom paid no heed to the overpowering fishy smell that pervaded the dank and gloomy cave. He had come here for a specific purpose and he was bent on achieving it.

"I have come to pay my respects to you," Chowmone Mangkhom replied. "I also bring you a message from the world of men." Chow Nong Long's curiousity was aroused. He asked the monk to take a seat and listened in rapt attention to the teachings of the Buddha. Chow Nong Long was so profoundly affected by the monk's talk that he promised not to eat any more humans. He personally escorted Chowmone Mangkhom to the shore.

"I shall come and visit you on the day of Satang," he told the monk. "I will come in human form."

"How will I recognize you?" Chomone Mangkhom asked. Chow Nong Long stretched himself out of the water to his full height and said, "You will know me!" The next minute he was gone. Chowmone Mangkhom went back to the monastery and recounted his amazing story to the villagers.

Five days later was Satang, the day when all the people gathered at the temple to pray. Chowmone Mangkhom was in the middle of his sermon when he noticed a handsome stranger seated at the rear corner of the hall. The monk noticed that the man kept brushing flies off his face. *That's him! The flies are attracted to his fishy smell.* After the sermon was over, the stranger got up and left. Chowmone Mangkhom followed him as he briskly walked towards the lake.

"Wait!" he shouted. "I know who you are." The stranger stopped in his tracks and smiled.

"I would like your permission to construct a temple near the lake to show the world that they have nothing to fear," the monk told him.

"You will know my answer tomorrow," Chow Nong Long replied.

That night people were woken up from their sleep when they felt the earth rumble and shake beneath them. In the morning they saw something strange. A huge rocky plateau was seen jutting out of the water in the middle of the lake.

The monk then built a beautiful temple on the plateau, which attracted pilgrims from far and wide. As for Chow Nong Long, he never was seen again.

Naka: Dragon; Satang: Holy day during period of retreat; Chowmone: Reverend

39

The Man Who Ate Three Pots of Rice

A very long time ago in a small little village there lived a poor farmer and his wife. They worked as hard as they possibly could but they never seemed to have enough money to spare. Their only son Samhai had such a voracious appetite that all their earnings went on food. Samhai grew up to be an exceptionally strong person and would eat nothing less than three pots of rice at one go.

"You eat so much that there's hardly any left for us," his father often scolded him, to no effect. At last his parents showed him the door. "It's best you go and earn your own living. We cannot support you any longer."

Feeling unwanted, Samhai tied his clothes into a bundle and left his home to go and seek his fortune. He had not gone far when he met a man who was dragging a heavy raft along the shore. Samhai struck up a conversation with the man whose name was Aipay. "My parents don't want me, so I am off to find my fortune," Samhai told him.

Aipay let go of the raft and said, "I shall go along with you. I too am an unwanted guest in my father's home." The two walked together until they met a man named Hapaksao, who was pulling five hundred logs tied together with ropes. They stopped to talk to him and when they told him where they were going, Hapaksao left his work to join them. The three young men kept walking till they came to a wide and swift flowing river.

Samhai suggested that they cross over to the other side. Aipay was a little apprehensive for he was not a very good swimmer. Hapaksao was doubtful too. The only one who did not seem unduly worried was Samhai. Taking out a stout rope from his bundle, he tied one end around his waist and waded into the water.

"Follow me. If you get tired you can hold on to the rope and I'll pull you across," Samhai told his companions. They all swam together with Samhai leading the way. The current was swift and Aipay was finding it difficult keeping up with the other two. When they were halfway across the river Aipay caught hold of the rope and let Samhai pull him along.

A little while later Hapaksao too caught hold of the rope and let Samhai pull him along with Aipay. Samhai did not seem to be tired at all. He swam with ease, pulling his two exhausted companions across the river. Just as he was about to reach the shore, Samhai saw an enormous fire-breathing dragon approaching them. Aipay and Hapaksao were so scared they almost let go off the rope.

"It's going to eat us!" Aipay and Hapaksao began to sob and panic.

"Quiet!" snapped Samhai. "You'll drive it away with all that noise." The two men shut their eyes tight and held on to the rope for dear life as Samhai swam towards the dragon.

The water was now shallow enough for Samhai to wade through. He caught hold of the dragon by the tail and flung it ashore with full force. Leaving Aipay and Hapakao lying dazed on the shore, Samhai rushed to the spot where the dragon lay and killed it with his machete. It had been a long time since the three had eaten and Samhai thought the dragon would make a good meal.

Aipay and Hapaksao went into the forest to get firewood while Samhai skinned and cut the dragon. He could see wisps of smoke in the distance. That meant there was a fire burning nearby. Hapaksao was the first to return with the firewood.

"Do you see that smoke?" Samhai asked him. "Go there and fetch a burning log to light the fire."

Hapaksao followed the smoke and came to a little bamboo house on stilts. "Who is it?" a voice called out from above. "What do you want?"

"I have come to ask for fire," Samhai replied. "I don't need much. Just a little piece of burning wood will do."

"If you want fire, come up and get it," the voice said.

Samhai climbed up the narrow steps and came face to face with Ya Phephai. She held a huge basket, with which she netted and imprisoned him in one swift movement.

"I've done nothing to you," Hapaksao cried out. "Why are you doing this to me?"

"Do you really wish to know?" the old woman cackled. "You'll stay there till I decide when to eat you. At the moment I'm not

Samhai rushed to the spot where the dragon lay and killed it with his machete.

hungry." She then cast a spell over the basket, so that her prisoner went off into a deep sleep and would not wake up unless she willed him to.

Aipay returned with the firewood but there was no sign of Hapaksao. Samhai had arranged the dragon meat on bamboo skewers and was fast losing his patience. "Go and find out what Hapakso is up to," Samhai told Aipay. "He should have been back long ago."

Following the direction of the smoke, Aipay reached Ya Phephai's house. "What do you want?" the old woman asked.

"I'm looking for my friend who came this way looking for fire," Aipay said. "Have you seen him?"

"I've seen no one, but if you want fire, you may have it," Ya Phephai replied. "Climb up the steps, my boy."

When Aipay reached the top of the steps he was caught and imprisoned inside a basket just like his friend before him. Ya Phephai could not believe her good luck. Two men waiting to be eaten and she did not even have to venture out of the house.

"Hee! Hee!" She laughed happily. "I'll eat this one after I've eaten the first. They smell so delicious already."

Seeing that his two companions had not yet returned, an angry Samhai decided to find out what was keeping them. "What idiots! They can't even carry out a simple task," he cursed aloud.

The old woman saw him from a distance. *Aah! The third one comes this way. This one is the fattest. His meat will last me many days.*

Samhai walked up to the house and looked at Ya Phephai who was standing on her little verandah. She seemed a harmless old woman.

"Have you seen my friends?" he asked.

The old woman put on an innocent face. "No, I have not seen any one," she said. "Why don't you come and sit by the fire?"

Samhai climbed up the narrow steps and came face to face with Ya Phephai. She stood in front of him with a basket in hand. With a sudden jerk, she brought the basket down on him, but

Samhai who could throw a fire dragon from water to land, was not to be caught so easily. He held her by her scanty topknot and gave her such a sound kick that she flew over the garden fence and died.

With the death of Ya Phephai, the spell she had cast over the two men was broken and they woke up. Samhai and his companions carried the dragon meat from the shore to Ya Phephai's house and roasted it over the burning fire.

Ya Phephai: Ogress, she demon

40

Chow Amasa

Chow Amasa was a conceited fellow who because of his strength, looked down on everyone else. One day he returned home in a jovial mood. He held one of the pillars of his house and shook it. The entire house rattled.

"Was that an earthquake?" the elder wife asked the younger one in alarm.

"Let's get out of here," the younger wife suggested. They left their cooking and ran out to the verandah.

Chow Amasa saw their frightened expressions and roared with laughter. "Do you see how strong I am? I can make the house shake with my bare hands. Come on you foolish women, tell me, have you seen anyone stronger than me?"

The elder wife pointed to an ant on the floor. "This ant is stronger than you. Although it is so tiny it can carry many times its own weight."

Chow Amasa did not like being compared to an ant. He crushed the tiny insect under his feet and slapped his two wives for being disrespectful towards him. The younger wife stood under a shady palm tree and cried her heart out.

"Don't cry!" she heard a voice behind her. It was a squirrel looking down at her from its perch. "Go tell your husband that there's someone who's stronger than him right here." She went and told her husband what the squirrel had told her. Brushing her aside, Chow Amasa stormed out to meet his challenger.

He caught hold of the squirrel's tail and gave it a yank. The squirrel dashed up the tree, pulling Chow Amasa along. With a flick of its tail, the squirrel hurled the great and mighty Chow Amasa into the sky and far, far away. Chow Amasa sailed through the air and landed with a thud on some thorny bushes in a strange land. Bruised and bleeding, he staggered to his feet and walked towards a nearby field to see a huge lion dragging a plough held by a giant. Chow Amasa watched in fascination as the giant and the lion zipped about at lightening speed. Before he knew what was happening, they zipped past him, leaving him buried under a mound of freshly ploughed earth.

The giant pulled Chow Amasa out and shook the mud off him, almost breaking his bones in the process. "It's a little man!" the giant exclaimed. "My children will be happy to have a new toy."

He took Chow Amasa home and handed him over to his children to play with. The giant's children were a rowdy bunch and tossed him about. When they grew tired of playing with him, they put him in a little pot and were about to cook him over the fire when their father came and stopped them. Luckily for Chow Amasa, the giant had a kind heart. He took Chow Amasa out of the pot and said, "Tell me if there is anything you want."

"I would like to go home," Chow Amasa replied. The giant felt sorry for Chow Amasa. He knew his children would sooner or later kill the little man if he kept him any longer.

"Go to my neighbour Chow Muksu and ask him to show you the way home," the giant said, pointing to a house in the distance. Chow Amasa walked up and down four hills to the neighbour's house and introduced himself.

"Can you help me find my way home?" He asked the giant. Chow Muksu took a closer look at him. "I suppose I may be able to help you little man," he said. "But first, let us have something to eat. My son has just come back from a hunt."

The giant's son was taller and heftier than his father. He seemed stronger too, for he carried an elephant across his shoulder as if it were a rabbit. Chow Amasa watched goggle eyed as both father and son tore large chunks of meat and ate the entire beast before his very eyes. Terrified that he might end up on the giant's dinner plate, Chow Amasa quaked in fear. A series of loud satisfied burps signalled the end of the meal. The giant now focused his attention on Chow Amasa. "Are you ready to go home?"

"Y—Yes," Chow Amasa stammered. "I really would like to leave." The giant picked him up and tied him to an arrow. Taking careful aim he let the arrow fly in the air. As he whistled through the air, Chow Amasa felt as though his entire body was being jabbed by millions of sharp needles. The arrow landed right at his doorstep. Chow Amasa called out to his wives, "Come here and untie me." His two wives came running and removed the strong ropes that bound their husband to the arrow.

Chow Amasa had learnt his lesson. He never boasted again and lived peacefully with his wives.

41

The Hunter & the Monks

A long time ago the abbot in charge of a monastery sent his pupils to the jungle and told them not to return until they had learnt to master their thoughts. The group of novice monks, five hundred strong, gathered on a hill top to practice the art of meditation. They were young and they were enthusiastic. They sat lotus posture, mindfully breathing in and breathing out till the time hunger proved stronger than will power.

They made an observation; an empty stomach cannot still the mind.

Abandoning their unfinished lesson they decided to return to the monastery. Having to face their teacher's wrath was better than dying of hunger, they reasoned.

Half way down they came across Ngachen the hunter, returning home from a hunt. He had a deer slung across his shoulder. "Where are you all heading for?" he asked.

"Back to the monastery," they told him.

"Will you be kind enough to tell the little stream you meet along the way that Ngachen needs water to wash and cook?" Muksu Ngachen said.

"Alright brother, we shall pass on your message to the little stream," they replied, wondering if he was mad.

They came to the little stream that Ngachen had told them about. "Little stream, Ngachen the hunter has summoned you to his home," they said in all politeness, even though they found it absurd.

The little stream gurgled loudly and with a sudden twist, changed its normal course and snaked its way up hill. The monks could not believe their eyes. They followed the little stream till they came to Ngachen's home. He was busy washing the meat and took no notice of the five hundred monks crowding around him.

"Ngachen," one of them said. "We want to know your secret. How did you get the stream to do your bidding?"

Ngachen looked up and smiled. "If you have the determination to succeed and believe in yourself you can achieve the impossible."

The monks were not satisfied with the explanation. "Teach us your secret," they implored.

Ngachen showed them the tallest manna tree in the jungle and told them to make a ladder tall enough to reach the top most branches. The monks got down to work and with the help of the ladder scaled the lofty branches of the manna tree. Ngachen chopped the ladder and used it as firewood to cook his meal.

The monks sat meditating for days without food and water till their stomachs rumbled in protest. The fruits of the manna tree were too tempting to resist and when they had eaten all the fruits, they chewed the leaves and ate the bark of the tree. The manna tree was stripped bare and before long the starving monks were hungry for more. They looked down at the little stream so very far away and could almost taste its cool refreshing water.

Desperation compelled a monk to try the impossible. *It is better to die trying than to stay here and die,* he pondered. Spreading out his arms he jumped off the branch. His robes ballooned out in the wind and he sailed freely, like a bird in the sky.

"I can fly!" he shouted joyfully, making a perfect landing and encouraging the others to follow him. And follow him they did, one after the other till the tree was truly bare. Ngachen gazed up at the manna tree and smiled in approval when he saw the monks flying down like a spray of ochre blossoms in the wind.

Manna tree: Jungle fruit tree

42

One Kilo Salt for One Gooseberry

There once lived a very poor man named Aiphan who went around begging for food. The villagers were kind and never refused him food. One day while resting under the cool shade of a gooseberry tree, a big fat gooseberry fell on him. He picked it up and examined it thoroughly from all possible angles. It was ripe and tempting, with not a blemish on it. Aiphan stopped short of taking a bite of the luscious fruit. *I'll need some salt to eat it with.* He put the fruit into his pocket and trotted off to the nearest house.

"Can I have a little salt?" he asked the kind old woman who gave him food every other day. She went in and returned with a handful of salt, which she emptied on to his begging cloth. Tying it into a bundle he went to the next house and asked, "Can you give me a little salt?" Here too he received another handful. He went to all the houses in the village and in this way managed to collect a kilo of salt. His bundle had become heavy and he was faced with a new problem. *Where shall I keep all this salt?* He walked around looking for a safe place to hide his salt and located a pond.

He carefully lowered his precious bundle into the pond and left it there for safekeeping. Feeling extremely pleased with himself for being so clever, Aiphan lay down under a tree and gloated over his new found wealth. It was impossible for him to sleep that night, for all he could think of was the bundle of salt that he had so carefully hidden. *What if someone came upon it and stole it? What shall I exchange it for?* All the years of begging did not disturb his sleep as much as owning a bundle of salt did. *Did all rich people have restless nights?*

Finally dawn approached. Aiphan hurried to the pond as soon as it was bright enough to see. He groped around in the water and could find nothing. *Where is my salt?* He frantically searched among the reeds and after what seemed an eternity caught something in his hand. Lifting it out of the water he recognized his begging cloth with four tight knots intact. Alas! There was nothing inside. Except for oozing water, the bundle was flat and empty. Someone had stolen his salt!

Aiphan looked this way and that. There was no one around except for a frog. "Oi frog! Was it you that stole my salt?" he accused the frog.

The startled frog tried to hop away, but Aiphan caught it and bound its legs with reed. He went to the neighbouring village and entered the gate of the first house he came across. Tying his frog to the pillar of the house, he climbed up the steps. Being a gracious host, the owner of the house offered him food and water. When Aiphan took his leave and went to the pillar, he found his frog missing. There was a big fat hen nearby.

"Your hen has gobbled up my frog," he accused the owner of the house. "Give me your hen in exchange or I will take you to court."

The owner of the house was a peace loving man. He did not want to get into an argument so he handed over his hen to Aiphan. Tucking the big fat hen under his arm, he walked happily along the way, till he came across a dead man lying on the wayside. Plucking the feathers off the hen, he threw them over the dead man and began to shout, "This man has stolen my hen! My one and only hen!" People came running out of their homes to find out what the commotion was all about.

"Why, it is my servant lying there," someone exclaimed. "What happened to him? How did he die?"

"All I know is that he has eaten my hen," Aiphan replied. "I'll have to take his body with me." The man was only too happy to oblige.

The elephant ran amuck, breaking the pots and causing a great deal of pandemonium among the crowds.

Aiphan lifted the dead man on his back and proceeded towards the elephant camp. He laid the body down and waited for the owner of the elephant to come. When he saw the owner approaching, Aiphan ran towards him crying, "Your elephant has killed my father. What shall I do?" The man offered to compensate for the loss. "Give me your elephant as compensation," Aiphan demanded. The man agreed and gave him the elephant.

Aiphan rode the elephant to the market place and dismounted near a row of potters who sat with their wares on display. The elephant ran amuck, breaking the pots and causing a great deal of pandemonium among the crowds. The angry potters caught the elephant and waited for the owner to show up. Aiphan of course did not go anywhere near the elephant. Instead, he picked up a piece of broken clay and walked away from the market place.

As he passed by a stream, he heard a bird's shrill cry. *"Khoorwak! Khoorwak!"* It trilled again and again. Thinking that the bird was making fun of him, Aiphan threw the piece of clay at the bird and killed it instantly. *"Khoorwak! Khoorwak!"* The sound was now coming from the piece of clay. He picked up his little weapon, which was now smeared with the bird's blood and went on his way.

By and by he came to the house of a rich man whose only daughter was busy weaving. Aiphan walked up to her from behind and said, "What beautiful designs you are weaving." He slyly wiped the blood off the clay on to her back without her being aware of it.

"Khoorwak! Khoorwak!" they both heard the sound. It seemed to be coming from the girl's back. *"Khoorwak! Khoorwak!"* It grew louder and louder. Alarmed, she stood up and dusted her back, trying to get rid of the sound but it kept calling, *"Khoorwak! Khoorwak!"*

"What evil spirit has possessed me?" she cried out. "Help me."

Aiphan was not one to miss an opportunity. "I may be able to help you," Aiphan said. "But, only if you promise me something in return. Will you marry me?"

The desperate girl had no choice. She was ready to promise anything if he was able to get rid of whatever was on her back. "All right, I'll marry you, but be quick about it!" she said. Aiphan took a clean wet piece of cloth and wiped the blood off the girl's back. There was no *'Khoorwak!'* sound after that.

The girl was so grateful that she married Aiphan the very next day. They lived happily in her father's house and in due course a son was born to them. Aiphan was a good father. He would strap the baby on his back and sing his favourite lullaby...

Makhaam hoi lung ku tok lung,
Ku tok khet, khet tok kai,
Kai tok patai, patai tok chang,
Chang tok moe, moe tok nok khoorwak,
Nok khoorwak tok mae mauh
Oye..Ooo, Ooo, Oye!

To this day, babies are lulled to sleep with this song. A translated version goes thus...
One gooseberry, one kilo of salt,
Salt for a frog, frog for a hen,
Hen for a corpse, corpse for an elephant,
Elephant for a pot, pot for a khoorwak bird,
Khoorwak bird for your mother,
Oye..Ooo, Ooo, Oye!

43

Pakkham the Jinx

A long time ago there lived a man by the name of Pakkham. He was going through hard times as he had lost all his money and the only thing left was a tiny piece of land. One day he went to his neighbour's house and borrowed an ox to plough his field. Once the ploughing was done he went to return the animal to its owner. He tied the animal to the pillar of the house and went up to chat with the man who was sitting on his verandah. That night the ox tugged at the rope and died of strangulation.

The next morning the neighbour came to him in a foul mood. "You have not returned my ox," he shouted angrily.

"Of course I returned your ox yesterday," Pakkham replied. "You saw me bringing it back and tying it to your pillar. Did you not?"

"You did not return it to me," the man insisted. "I want my ox back." The two of them argued on and on until they decided to go to the king to seek justice.

Along the way they came across a man who was trying in vain to round up his horses, which ran in different directions. "Come and help me round them up," the man called out to them.

Pakkham picked up a stone and threw it at a runaway horse, aiming to send it back to the herd. The stone hit the horse's eye and blinded it. The owner was livid. "Look at what you did! You've blinded my horse. Now pay for it."

"I was only trying to help you round up your horses," Pakkham replied. "It was an accident." The man was unwilling to listen to him. He too accompanied them to seek justice.

It was a hot afternoon and Pakkham was very thirsty. He saw a pregnant woman sitting on her verandah. "Can you give me some water?" he asked her. The woman got up and picked up a pot of water to give it to him, but she slipped and fell. The baby born to her did not survive.

"It's all your fault," she wailed. "You killed my baby and you will have to pay for it. I will take you to the king." She too joined the group. Now there were three people against Pakkham.

As they continued on their way, Pakkham was sinking deeper and deeper into depression. *How will I repay all of them when I have no money? It would be better if I were dead.* They were now walking along the riverbank. Right below them on the edge of the river was a fisherman tending to his dying father. Pakkham jumped off the bank in a bid to end his life. Unfortunately for him, he landed on the chest of the fisherman and killed him instantly.

"You killed my father," the fisherman accused him. Seeking justice, he too went along with them to the king. Upon reaching the palace they were taken to the king's court. The king gave a patient hearing to the various complaints against Pakkham and first of all summoned the neighbour whose ox had died.

"Did you or did you not see this man bring in your ox?" he asked.

"Yes, your majesty," the neighbour replied.

"Where did he leave the ox?" the king asked.

"He tied it to the pillar instead of handing it over to me," the neighbour replied.

The king gave his verdict. "You are wrong in accusing him. If you saw him tie your ox to your pillar, it means he has returned the animal to you. How can he be held responsible for what occurred in your compound afterwards?" The neighbour had nothing to say to that.

It was the horse sellers' turn to face the king. "Take this stone and throw it at the horse standing outside. Hit it in the eye and blind it," the king commanded. "If you miss its eye and hit it elsewhere I will have you thrown in prison." The horse seller protested.

"It is not possible for me to hit him in the eye, your majesty. I might miss it."

"Exactly!" said the king. "This man did not intentionally blind your horse. He was only trying to help you." The horse seller saw the truth in the king's words.

To the woman who lost her child, the king said, "How was he to know that you were about to deliver? He only asked for water. No one forced you to give it so you cannot blame him for your misfortune." The woman realized her folly.

The king now looked at the fisherman. "How can you blame him for your father's death? You both were down below and not visible to anyone." Turning to the rest the king asked them if they saw the fisherman from above.

"No, your majesty, we did not see anyone from above," they replied. The case went in favour of Pakkham. The king gave them a piece of advice, "Never be hasty in blaming others for your misfortune."

Pakkham went home a relieved man and the others much wiser.

Legends/Beliefs/Rituals

Khamtis believe in the concept of a parallel universe populated with spirits of all kinds, from the benign to the harmful. They also have the in-betweens, those that alternate between human and spirit form and practice sorcery.

PHEE TASAY MANJA: These are greedy little spirits that are about three feet high and thrive on filth. They thrive in marshy areas and dirty places eating filth. At night they resemble little balls of fire, floating around in groups. Considered harmless, they can cause stomach upsets and nameless aches and pains. During the night they croak like frogs and it only takes a little shouting to quiten them.

PHEE SANKHENG: Spirits of those recently buried or those that have had accidental deaths. They are tormented souls who are still attached to the material world or those whose funeral rites have not been properly observed. They live in the cemeteries. New entrants are bullied by the older inhabitants in their own parallel spirit world. Sometimes they are seen as charging bulls.

PHEE SAKAK KHAM: Spirit of the jungle, it imitates the sound of wild elephants on a rampage although nothing can be seen. Sometimes trees appear to be rushing towards the victim. Is an invisible entity, capable of causing death.

PHEE THUN: Forest spirits or forest people. There are two types. There are the tiny ones that are about a foot high, red skinned and very shy. They have red hair and feet that are turned backwards. They are normally seen near streams and pools in the forest, catching and eating live fish. If they hear any sound they immediately run for cover. In the early nineteen sixties five temple boys went to a stream for fishing and saw four little red men bending over the stream, chattering away in their squeaky voices. As soon as the little red beings became aware of being watched, they ran into some nearby bushes and disappeared. Then there are the giants among them. They are about eight to ten feet tall, very dark complexioned, hooked nosed and have long unkempt hair. They roam the rivers and streams looking for fish, crabs and snails.

PUHSU: Similar to witches and werewolves, *Puhsus* are masters in the art of deception. There is a saying: 'If air can pass through the tiniest crack so can a *Puhsu*.' Victims of *Puhsus* suffer from mysterious illnesses and sudden death, while family members report seeing shadowy figures and hearing unearthly noises in their home. The victim is carried off by enthusiastic *Pushus* who leave behind a log of wood or anything available as replacement. To human eyes it would appear that the person is still there. Children below seven and animals are the only ones able to see *Puhsus* in their true form. Dogs, cats and cattle go into a frenzy when *Puhsus* are in the vicinity.

Puhsus are ordinary human beings during the day, but as night approaches they cannot suppress the urge to wander about on their flying chariot called "*OT-ET*" because of the creaky "OT-ET" sound it makes while airborne. They leave their bodies behind in bed while they make their nightly rounds in the shape of animals or even the form of another person. While in the process of shape shifting, the face is said to distort and elongate. Frightful as it may be for an observer, it is a time when they are most vulnerable and unable to defend themselves from attack. Sometimes shape shifting is beyond their control. It is probably for this reason that *Puhsus* sleep tucked under a sheet like mummies even in hot and humid weather, because they fear others might discover their secret.

True story: A learned monk would often notice that one of his temple boys was always missing from the monastery at night. Very early one morning he noticed the boy entering the monastery gate. Confronting him, he asked him where he had been all night. The boy said he had been to the most beautiful places on earth. He had played in gardens filled with all kinds of flowers, rowed down silvery streams and walked in beautiful meadows. The monk gave the boy a bundle of sticks with white paper flags pasted on them. He told the boy to take the bundle with him that night and plant one flag in every place he'd been to. The boy followed the instructions and came back the following morning empty handed.

"Let's go and see the beautiful places you visited last night," the monk told the boy. The monk and the boy then went out together. The first flag was found standing on a pile of cow dung. Some were found under houses, in dirty pools of water, piles of rotting garbage, pigsty and such like. The boy was stunned. "How did the flags come to be in such filthy places?" he asked. The monk gave him this answer. "Whatever you saw at night was a mirage created by the devil, who controls your soul. You have chosen to follow him." The boy was asked to leave the monastery.

True story: Ya Lake or iron lady as she was fondly known in the village died at the ripe old age of ninety. When she was around eighteen years of age she suddenly fell ill and was on the verge of death. As she lay dying, her parents called for the same monk to pray for her recovery. The monk told them that it was the work of the Puhsus and sat down to chant some very powerful mantras. As if in a dream, she saw a man and his wife, known to be puhsus from her village, enter her room with two baskets of fresh meat, still dripping with blood. The next day Ya lake woke up perfectly fine. In fact, after that incident she never suffered so much as a headache or even a body ache her entire life. She jokingly used to attribute her good health to the *Puhsus* who she thinks may have relaced her flesh with that of buffalo meat.

PHEE KHO: Greedy spirits that reside in people who are by nature greedy, jealous and covetous. In most cases the *Phee Kho* attaches itself to very poor people who cannot afford a decent meal and grudge others who do. The host to the *Phee Kho* reffered to as *Phee Nip* will unknowingly possess the evil eye, causing severe stomach cramps, indigestion, diarrhoea and vomiting to others who eat in the presence of the *Phee Nip* without offering him/her any food. It is a rule among the Khamtis who eat in public view to first take a small portion of food and throw it away as a symbolic offering to the *Phee Kho*. When babies and small children suffer stomach cramps, a little bit of every food item that the child eats is offered to the *Phe Kho* along with the lighting of incense sticks and chanting. The food is discarded outside the house.

KHON YON: When we miss a favourite article or a person and we want it back desperately but are unable to, our *khon* or soul pines for the lost article/person and our health deteriorates. Sometimes when the pain of seperation is unbearable, the *khon* leaves the body to go in search of the departed companion, never to return, and the person dies. In order to bring the person back to normal health it is essential to bring the *khon* back. Khamtis have a special method by which they achieve that. A *khuk* or fishing basket is filled with the clothes of the sick person along with a little cooked rice and some hard boiled eggs. This is then taken to the spot where the sick person first felt a sudden wave of shock leading to his/her illness. Usually it is the site of accident or the grave of his/her companion. The person holding the *khuk* drags it all around the place, as though fishing and coaxes the *khon* to return home. *"Are you there? Come, let's go back home together."* When this is done, the *khuk* is covered with white muslin and taken home.

When the cloth is removed and the *khuk* is emptied out, the *khon* is found inside, in the form of a frog or a grasshopper or any other insect. It is taken out and put over the sick person. The eggs are cut into half and the yolk is smeared on the forehead, knees and elbows of the patient. A little is fed to him/her and the rest is given to the children gathered there. Once the *khon* is back, the person makes a quick recovery.

When there is a death in the family, the clothes of all the family members are put into a *khuk* and it is dragged around the dead body lest any *khons* be attracted to the dead person. The *khuk* is then covered with white muslin and kept aside untouched. The clothes are taken out only after all the ceremonies are over.
PHEE NAM: Water spirit named Nang Munimikhla, who has long and luxuriant hair from which water flows. She resides in the river but often wanders around the land invisible. Sometimes we unknowingly brush against her while she strolls along or we show disregard for her. As a consequence we suffer from frozen shoulder, tennis elbow and other aches and pains. People therefore pray to her by pouring water in front of their door and asking the Phee Nam for forgiveness for unintentionally brushing against her.
LIC SANGKEN: Every Sangken or the New Year, which falls around April 14th. Chow Khunkiew leaves his abode in the Saupha Mengmo hill from where he keeps a watch over the world and comes down to collect souls to contain the population on earth. He comes riding on a creature, holding certain articles in his hands, deciding who to punish and who to reward. He is the lord of war, famine, disease, death and suffering. He scatters the seed of new disease along with the seeds that cure them. It is for the earth people to discover the cures for the diseases that are sown, for every disease has a cure to it. As he moves, he sweeps the souls of the dead along with him, sometimes in large numbers. Depending on the mode of his transport and the article held in his left hand, the predictions for the year ahead are made by the astrologers.

If Chow Khunkiew appears on a winged horse it means that Sangken will be earlier than usual. It also means that whatever is started will be completed in good time. When Chow Khunkiew appears on a caterpillar, Sangken will be later than usual and everything will take time to be completed. Things will move very slowly. When he rides a buffalo it predicts a year of heavy rainfall. A cow signifies plenty of sunshine and a dragon means rain, storms and floods. When he rides on Garuda, be certain of strong winds and cyclones. The snail would mean that projects undertaken that year would be unsuccessful. Riding a snake signifies a fruitful year for farmers as well as widespread cases of stomach ailments.

More important than the mode of transport is the article, which Chow Khunkiew's holds in his left hand. Holding a flower vase signifies a peaceful year ahead. A sword means war, fights, unrest. A spear is a sure sign of success in everything. A waterpot means there will be ways and means to overcome suffering. Carrying fire signifies accidents caused by fire. The hook means there will be treachery. When Chow Khunkiew clutches his stomach it means there will be famine.

CHOWSANG PHAUMPUK: The eternal protector of the earth. Legend has it that whenever there was a festival or a marriage or some important occasion, Chow Khunsong the god of destruction, would appear uninvited and make a nuisance of himself. Fed up with his ways, Chowsang Phaumpuk decided to punish him. He took the skin of a smelly and rotting dead dog and tied it around the neck of Chow Khunsong to keep him away. Chow Khunsong could not remove the offensive skin and neither could anyone excepting Chowsang Phaumpuk, who only did so after the festivities were over.

People are still wary of Chow Khunsong who plays spoilsport by bringing wind and rain, ruining their plans so they turn to Chowsang Phaumpuk for his divine intervention. Food is prepared by pre-pubescent girls or old people (who have given up worldly pleasures to spend most of their time in meditation) and placed on a covered platform by the river bank. If he is pleased with the offering, be assured that on that particular day or days, the weather will be perfect, even if there has been incessant rain for days. If on the other hand, Chowsang Phaumpuk is offended due to some neglect on the part of those who have prepared the offering, he will show his displeasure by sending a terrible storm.

KHON KHOW: The soul of the rice plant. It lives in the paddy fields among the rice and is responsible for a bountiful crop. The Khamtis revere it. When harvest time approaches, the mistress of the house chooses a sturdy rice plant to represent the khon khow and leaves it untouched till all the rice has been harvested. When the entire crop has been harvested, she finally uproots the khon khow and says, "Come, let us go home." She puts it in her basket and covers it with white muslin. She carries the basket strapped to her back and looks neither left nor right while she walks home. She doesn't utter a word either. If anyone should speak to her, she will not reply lest the khon khow leaves her and goes to the other person. When people see a woman carrying a basket with a rice plant in it, they don't talk to her because they know she will not reply.

Once she reaches home, she opens her 'Ye khow' or granary and taking the khon khow, plants it on the top of the mound of grain. There it stays, guarding the food supply of the owners. Each time grain is taken out of the granary, the mistress says 'Che-chook! Che-chook!' and a fistful of grain is put back for the khon khow. This is to ensure that the khon khow does not leave the granary and there is no shortage of food in the house.

PHEE CHOW MAUNG: The spirit guardian of the village, he lives at the entrance of the village in a house constructed especially for him by the villagers. Every time people pass by the Phee Chow Maung's abode either on their way in or out of the village they pray to him for peace and protection. Once a year the villagers get together and offer food and prayers to the Phee Chow Maung.

If there has been a theft, the people concerned pray to him, hoping that he reveals the identity of the thief so that justice can be served. If animals are lost, the owners pray to Phee Chow Maung to help find their animals again.